Mills & Boon Classics

A chance to read and collect some of the best-loved novels from Mills & Boon – the world's largest publisher of romantic fiction.

Every month, four titles by favourite Mills & Boon authors will be re-published in the *Classics* series.

A list of other titles in the *Classics* series can be found at the end of this book.

Roberta Leigh

FORGOTTEN MARRIAGE

MILLS & BOON LIMITED
LONDON · TORONTO

First published 1959 as
MEMORY OF LOVE by Janey Scott
Australian copyright 1978
Philippine copyright 1978
This edition 1978

ISBN 0 263 72774 2

Set in 11 on 13pt. Pilgrim

*Made and Printed in Great Britain by
C. Nicholls & Company Ltd
The Philips Park Press, Manchester*

CHAPTER ONE

THE girl opened her eyes and stared at the ceiling. A hammer seemed to be beating in her head and she found it impossible to focus. But curiosity forced her to keep her eyes open and, as the grey mist thinned, she saw a large metallic machine at the side of the bed and, beyond it, a blur of white. She tried to remember where she was but found it difficult to concentrate, and with a sigh, allowed her lids to droop and consciousness to recede.

When she awoke the second time her head was clearer and her vision normal. She looked around the room: austerely furnished, it was obviously in a hospital or nursing home.

She tried to sit up, but her body would not obey the command of her brain. Panic-stricken, she wondered if she was paralysed, but as she thought it, she realised she was clenching and unclenching her hands. Some of her panic ebbed and carefully she turned her head. It moved from side to side and the relief was so enormous it made her feel weak. She had been in some sort of accident—that much was clear—and was now recovering.

She paused in her thoughts, waiting for memory to fill her mind with people and places; a particular person and a special place. But nothing came. No names or faces; no house or apartment.

It was then that panic returned and would not be stilled. What had happened to her? Who was she? Where did she belong? She was gripped by a wave of fear so strong that it brought her into a sitting position.

"Who am I?" she said aloud. "What do I look like?" Hearing her voice increased her feeling of unreality and heightened her panic. "Who am I?" she wailed again, and started to cry. As her sobs filled the room, the door opened and a nurse hurried across to her.

"Now, now, we can't have this," a lilting Welsh voice soothed. "What's the matter?"

"Who am I?" the girl begged. "What's happened to me?"

"You're in Fairview Hospital. You were brought here after the crash."

"What crash?"

"The plane crash. You were coming from South Africa. Don't you remember?"

"No! I don't remember anything. My head—everything's going round." She struggled to sit up straighter, but the nurse restrained her.

"There's no call to get upset. So you have a head injury and it must have affected your memory. It often happens. But you'll soon start remembering. The main thing is not to worry."

The girl put her hand to her head and felt the thick bandage. "What's my name? I don't even remember that!"

"You will," the nurse soothed. "Just don't get excited, or you'll make yourself worse."

The girl swallowed and made an effort at control. "Could you at least tell me my name?"

"It's Sharon Peters, Mrs. Sharon Peters."

"Sharon Peters—Sharon." The girl repeated the name slowly. "It means nothing to me. It could belong to anyone."

"Well, it belongs to you! There's no doubt about that."

"Did you say—Mrs. Peters? Then I must have a husband! Was he in the plane crash with me?"

"Not as far as I know. But the house doctor has all the facts about you. I'm only a temporary—standing in for Nurse Marks, who's on holiday."

"I see." Sharon stared at the band of gold on her left hand. It was a slim, narrow hand with tapering fingers and soft skin, and she studied it as though it would yield some clue to her identity. But it remained the hand of a stranger, and she looked up again.

The nurse smiled. "Feeling better?"

"Not much. It's peculiar not knowing who you are." She laughed shakily. "I don't even know what I look like!"

"Then you're in for a pleasant surprise! You're as pretty as a picture."

"Do you have a mirror?"

"I'll try to find a hand one. But take my word for it, you're very beautiful."

Reassured, Sharon's thoughts went to the accident. "Was it a bad crash?" she asked.

"I'm afraid so. You're lucky to be alive."

"Were many people killed?"

"Quite a few," the nurse said evasively.

"But wasn't there anyone on the plane who knew me? If I could talk to someone who was there, who travelled with me—"

"You were travelling alone, that's what the airline said. And there's no one to whom you can talk, I'm afraid. It was a terrible crash and you should thank God you're alive."

Unspoken horror was implicit in the words and Sharon began to tremble. The nurse felt it and immediately became professional.

"You've nothing to worry about, Mrs. Peters. You weren't badly injured, and once you've recovered from your concussion you'll be as right as rain."

"But my memory—"

"Will come back as soon as you're over the shock, I promise you."

But the promise was to no avail. Two days passed and Sharon was still unable to recollect any details of her life.

On the morning of the third day the nurse placed a mirror in her hand, but she lacked the courage to look at it. Would the shock of seeing her face bring back her memory, or would she merely be staring at the face of a stranger?

"Come on now," the nurse chided. "You'll like what you see, providing you make allowance for the bandage."

With a trembling hand Sharon lifted the mirror and looked into it. Large, dark blue eyes, set wide apart in a heart-shaped face, looked back at her. A small, full mouth was startlingly red against the pallor of her skin, while her hair, or the little she could see of it beneath the disfiguring bandage, was so fair as to be almost silver.

She let the mirror drop to the counterpane. She knew her name, and she knew what she looked like; yet still no chord of memory echoed in her brain. She was like a doll that had just been manufactured. A product of the hospital, she thought fancifully, and one that had no buyer. Perhaps they would let her stay here for ever, allow her to live and die in antiseptic limbo.

"Didn't I tell you how pretty you were?" the nurse smiled, taking back the mirror.

"Pretty lonely," Sharon retorted, and was surprised by the edge of sharpness in her response. At least it meant she wasn't a dullard. Her past was lost, but if she had some intelligence she might be able to work out the future for herself. As she thought of the empty years ahead, a familiar sensation of panic rose in her. The nurse recognised the signs.

"Don't start having hysterics on me," she said cheerfully, "or I'll get a rocket from Staff Nurse for giving you a mirror."

"It has nothing to do with what I look like," Sharon said impatiently. "It's just this feeling so alone. Like a newborn child who's born an orphan."

"You're no orphan. Your family have been enquiring about you ever since the crash."

"My family?" Sharon gaped at her. "Why didn't you tell me I have a family? Why did no one mention their names? If I'd seen them I might have remembered again. You had no right to keep them away from me."

"You'll have to take that up with Dr. Farley. He's the one who issued the order."

"Then ask him to come here at once. I've never heard of such—"

"Before or after your visitor?" the nurse cut in.

Sharon gasped. "What visitor? Why didn't you tell me someone's waiting to see me?"

"I'm telling you now."

"Who is it?"

"A man. He'll tell you himself who he is. He's called every day since you were brought here. I'll tell him to come in."

"No!" The word burst from Sharon's lips almost of its own volition, the result of a deep-seated fear even greater than her fear of remaining ignorant of her past. Who was this man who had constantly enquired about her? Was he a friend or a lover? Beads of perspiration broke out on her forehead and with a shaking hand she rubbed them away.

"Tell him to come back later. I want to talk to Dr. Farley first."

"And leave your visitor kicking his heels in the corridor for hours? That isn't a very friendly thing to do."

"Then tell him to go away. I can't see anyone."

"You'll want to see him," the nurse laughed. "He's what you might call a real dreamboat!"

With a knowing wink she whisked out and Sharon stared at the door, her heart beating wildly. Almost immediately it opened again and a tall, broad-shouldered man strode in.

"Hello, Sharon. How are you feeling?"

Sharon swallowed hard. She had no sense of recognition and was overwhelmed by despair.

"I've brought you some flowers," he went on, setting a bouquet on the dressing table.

"Who are you?" Her voice was a whisper.

"Adam Peters."

"You're not—" She put a hand to her mouth. "But I don't know you; I can't remember your face. You're not my husband?"

"No," he said flatly, "I'm not. And you needn't be upset because you don't remember me. This is the first time we've met."

"Oh!" She smiled uncertainly, but there was no answering smile on his face and she looked down. "You have the same surname as mine: does that mean you're a relative?"

"You were my brother's wife."

Her head jerked up. "Your brother! Where is he? Why hasn't—" Her voice began to shake. "Was he killed in the crash? Is that what you're afraid to tell me?"

"No. Rufus died in a car accident in South Africa six months ago. You were on your way to visit us. I'm afraid all your luggage has been lost, but this letter was found in the pocket of your suit. You might like to read it."

With trembling fingers Sharon took the letter. The edges of it were stained with blood, but the writing was unmarked and the gist of it was clear. It was signed Adele Peters and welcomed Sharon to Green Spinney Lodge.

She raised her head. "This is from Rufus's mother, isn't it?"

He nodded and moved to the window. His profile outlined against the light, was angular and forbidding. He had an abundance of black hair, well-groomed and shiny, which was as much an indication of his personality as his beautifully tailored suit and highly polished shoes: a man of means who liked the best, and got it. He turned to face her and she noticed his eyes. They were grey as an iceberg and just as cold.

"There's no point in our discussing the present situation," he said, "until you remember the past. But one thing I will say: you won't get a penny out of me if you let my mother down."

"Let your mother down?" She stared at him uncomprehendingly. "Why should I do that?"

"Because it's a habit of yours to let people down. But of course you don't remember!" A grim smile twisted his face. "I've spoken to Dr. Farley and he says there's no reason why you can't leave here. The only treatment you need is rest. I'll make arrangements to pick you up tomorrow afternoon. Would you like a nurse to accompany you on the journey?"

"Is it far?" Sharon asked.

"A couple of hours by car."

"I'm sure I'll be able to manage on my own." She gave him a nervous smile. "I won't be on my own anyway. You'll be with me."

"Yes." It was a terse agreement. "Until tomorrow, then."

The door closed behind him and she gazed at it as if his image was imprinted on the woodwork. What a strange man! He had spoken to her as if he hated her. Yet how could he hate her when he had met her for the first time today? But everything he said had been redolent of hostility and disbelief. It was almost as if he doubted her loss of memory. That he thought it simply a blind to cover—what?

She closed her eyes. It was useless to try and solve a mystery where perhaps none existed. She was Sharon Peters, widow of a man she did not remember, in a country she did not know, about to stay with a woman she had never met. It was a poor collection of facts, but the only one she had.

In the early afternoon of the next day a nurse brought her a parcel. Inside were some clothes and a note from her mother-in-law: "I'm afraid these may not be your style and they probably won't fit, but I hope they'll do until you're strong enough to shop for some proper ones."

Sharon held up a blue dress. It was a fine silk material and of good cut, but far too large.

"What a gorgeous colour," the nurse commented from the door. "It'll match your eyes."

"I'd rather it fitted my figure!"

Shakily Sharon started to put on the clothes. The effort was tiring and she was still not completely dressed when the nurse returned to say Mr. Peters wanted to know how much longer she would be.

"Another five minutes."

"You can't go without doing your hair," the nurse exclaimed. "I've been dying to get my fingers on it ever since we took off the bandages." She sat Sharon on a chair and began to brush the long, silvery strands. "I've never seen such a colour," she admired. "And it will look even better when you're not so pale. There, I've given you a centre parting and let it fall naturally. You have real waves, Mrs. Peters, not permed ones!"

"My hair's always been easy to manage," Sharon said, then stopped. "Now what made me say that?"

"A sort of reflex action in the brain, I should think. Don't look so startled; it's a sign your memory's returning." The nurse proffered her arm. "Come along, I'll see you down to the car."

Slowly Sharon went along the corridor to the lift. As it descended to the lobby her heart began to thump and she chided herself for being foolish. Although she was going to stay with strangers, they were still her husband's family—she must remember that. Even though she could not remember her husband!

At the entrance, Adam Peters was standing beside a grey Bentley. He waited while Sharon said goodbye to the nurse and helped her into the front seat before taking his place behind the wheel. He did not speak until they left the hospital some miles behind them.

"How does it feel to be out and about?" he asked.

"Strange but wonderful." She looked through the window and in the pane saw her reflection with the blue silk dress hanging on her in folds.

"Why are you smiling?" he asked abruptly.

"At the sight I look! It was thoughtful of your mother to send me a dress, but I'm afraid it's rather big."

"Don't worry. She'll buy you some clothes as soon as you're fit enough to travel to London."

"I wasn't hinting!"

"I'm glad to hear it," he said coldly.

Deflated by his tone, Sharon did not answer. Once more they drove in silence, leaving London behind and entering a greener world, where it was easy to see it was spring. The hedges were covered with small white flowers and the trees were heavily laden with blossom. She was startled when his voice interrupted her thoughts.

"Different scenery from South Africa, isn't it?"

"I suppose so. I can't remember."

"Do you mean your mind's a complete blank?"

"Yes. If you'd told me you were my husband, I'd have believed you."

"I'm sure your instinct would have told you I wasn't. If Rufus attracted you, I certainly wouldn't."

"Were you so different?" she asked.

"Yes."

"In what way?" He gave an almost inaudible sigh of exasperation, and she said quickly, "I'm not asking out of idle curiosity, Mr. Peters. But I'd like to know what my husband looked like, particularly as I'm going to stay with your mother."

His hands tightened on the wheel. "Of course. You're quite right."

"I know it must hurt you to talk about him, but—"

"Forget it," he said abruptly. "I'll show you some photographs of him when we get home. Then you can judge for yourself how different we were. Rufus was twenty-six when you married him and twenty-eight when he was killed in a road accident in Cape Town. That's where you first met."

"Did he work there?"

"No. He was working for an uncle on a fruit farm and met you when he was holidaying at the Cape. It was a whirlwind romance, I believe."

His tone made it clear he wished she'd been whirled away in another direction, but she ignored it.

"What happened after I married him? Did we live on the farm?"

The man laughed harshly. "You wouldn't even give it a try, according to Rufus. You had a flat in the city and led a rather active social life."

"And?" she said when he stopped speaking and gave no indication of continuing. "Please tell me anything else you know. I'd like to know as much about myself as possible."

"I don't know much more. Let's hope your memory will return and you'll be able to tell me a few things." He reached into his breast pocket, took out a narrow crocodile case and extracted a slim cigar. "I'm afraid I can't offer you a cigarette."

She smiled. "I don't feel as if I want one."

For the first time his face relaxed its grim lines. "Then don't encourage yourself! Your vices will come home to roost soon enough."

"I wonder if I have many?"

He glanced at her sideways but made no comment, and Sharon closed her eyes. The smooth rhythm of the car lulled her to sleep and she didn't awake until the Bentley swung through large, wrought-iron gates and purred along a curving drive. She saw a spinney whose trees thinned out to disclose a lake, and behind it, on the far bank, stood a large and imposing Georgian house. Lights gleamed through the long, graceful windows and the mahogany door at the top of the shallow steps was flanked by slender white columns that reminded her of stories she had read about the American Deep South.

But nothing was more English than the panelled hall she entered, with its graceful sweep of staircase and Chippendale furniture.

"We'd better go into the drawing room," her brother-in-law said, and led the way towards a door off the hall.

Suddenly the floor wavered in front of her and she clutched at his arm. For an instant he stiffened, then he held her other arm and steadied her.

"Shall I carry you?" he offered.

"No, thank you. I just felt faint for a second."

He looked down at her. "You haven't been out of bed long. Perhaps you'd prefer to go straight to your room and meet my mother tomorrow?"

"I'd much rather meet her now."

"Then come and sit in here while I fetch her."

He guided Sharon to an armchair in a long, L-shaped room. When the door closed behind him she sat up straighter and glanced around. The windows were hung with brocade curtains, their muted pastel shades picking out the colours of the Aubusson carpet on the floor and the faded yet still beautiful tapestry that covered the settees. It was much more luxurious than anything she had envisaged, and she was dismayed at the prospect of living among people who were used to this type of environment. And if Adam Peters was an example of Rufus's family, the sooner she left here, the better!

The impending meeting with her mother-in-law—to which she had looked forward since the previous day—was now something she dreaded. She sprang to her feet, intent on escape.

But it was too late. The door opened and Adam and an elderly woman entered. Sharon had time to notice that the woman was small and plump with a gentle face and faded brown hair, before she was enfolded in soft arms.

"My dear child, how lovely to have you with us! I can't tell you how pleased I am." The woman drew back and looked at her son. "Ring for tea, darling. I'm sure you must both be longing for some." She crossed to the sofa, keeping hold of Sharon's hand. "There's no need to look frightened. You're among your family now and we'll look after you."

"You're very kind." Sharon's voice was thick with tears as she sat beside her mother-in-law. "I'm sure my—I'm sure Rufus told me about you, but I can't remember."

"Don't worry about it. You're here now and you'll be able to get to know us for yourself. If Rufus could have been with you it would have been perfect." A spasm of pain crossed Mrs. Peters's face. "I still can't believe he's dead. He was always so full of fun and high spirits."

Sharon touched the plump shoulder. "It must be painful for you to remember."

"Memories are all I have left."

"And I have none." Unconsciously Sharon clasped her hands tightly on her lap to stop them from trembling.

"I suggest we keep off the past, Mother." Adam came into the conversation, his eyes fixed on Sharon's hands. "The first thing for Sharon to do is to get to know us. After all, we might be the biggest villains unhung."

"What a silly thing to say!" his mother expostulated. You'll scare the poor girl out of her wits."

"I couldn't be afraid in a lovely house like this," Sharon said with a smile. "It speaks for itself."

"I'm sure it does."

The edge to Adam's voice told Sharon he was referring to something else, though she had no way of guessing what.

"When you said you were bringing me to Green Spinney Lodge," she said hastily, "I thought it was a cottage."

"A thirty-roomed cottage," he replied. "I can supply you with an inventory if you like."

"Adam!" Mrs. Peters looked reproving. "That isn't a very good joke."

The man opened his mouth as though to speak, then closed it again and crossed to the door. "If you'll excuse me, I have some work to do. I'll see you both later."

The moment they were alone Mrs. Peters edged

closer to Sharon. "Don't take any notice of Adam, my dear. He still feels Rufus's death very badly. There was nearly seven years' difference between them and Adam always played the big brother."

Sharon sighed. "I suppose I remind him of things he'd rather forget."

"Adam will never forget Rufus. He doesn't talk about him, but I know he broods."

Once again Sharon sensed something deeper in these words than appeared on the surface. But before she could glean any more, a maid wheeled a tea trolley into the room.

"Mr. Adam said he won't come in for tea. He's gone down to the home farm to have a word with Wilkins."

"Thank you, Beryl. My daughter-in-law will pour for me."

Nervously Sharon lifted the heavy silver teapot. "At least I haven't forgotten how to pour tea," she remarked with a smile. "It's so frightening not to know anything about myself."

"Try not to worry, my dear. I'm sure your memory will come back as suddenly as it went."

Sharon sighed. "I hope so. At the moment I must seem rather unfeeling when you talk about your—about Rufus."

"No one looking at you could accuse you of being unfeeling." Mrs. Peters accepted her cup. "You're not a bit as I imagined you. You're younger and more—more gentle. But then Rufus always had perfect taste."

Sharon dropped her gaze to her lap. "You're very complimentary."

"I am honest. It is an old woman's privilege."

When they had finished tea, Mrs. Peters offered to show Sharon to her room.

"It was thoughtless of me not to have asked if you wanted to go there when you first arrived. But I was so excited to see you that I forgot."

Walking with a slight limp, she led the way to the second floor. Bedrooms ran along either side of a wide corridor and she traversed its entire length before entering a room at the end. It was large and had a magnificent view of the lake and small wood. But it was not the scenery so much as the room itself that held Sharon's attention, for it had obviously belonged to Rufus. On the walls hung football pennants, models of aircraft and cartoons of famous cricketers. Battered textbooks overflowed the bookshelves and were ranged along the dressing table, side by side with a profusion of photographs. Quickly she scanned them, seeing Rufus in white shorts and sweater, then in cricket flannels and finally in tropical kit.

"As you see, I've put you in Rufus's room," Mrs. Peters said, picking up a photograph and handing it to Sharon. "This is the most recent one." She hesitated. "Does it bring back any memories?"

Sharon looked intently at the fair-haired man smiling back at her. There was no resemblance to Adam in the boyish face and careless pose.

"I'm afraid not," she said, and glanced along the bookshelves. But the schoolboy classics and sporting annuals gave no indication of the character of the man she had married.

"If you'd like me to tell you about Rufus, I'll gladly do so," Mrs. Peters offered.

"That's very kind of you, but—" Sharon put her hand to her head. "It's all so confusing. I don't quite know where I am."

"You're among your family—that's all you need think about. Why don't you lie down until dinner? Or would you prefer to have it up here on a tray?"

"Please don't go to such trouble, I'll be fine once I've had a rest."

"Good. You'll find a change of clothes in the wardrobe and some lingerie in the drawer. Tomorrow, if you feel strong enough, we can go to London and get you some new clothes."

"Not for the moment," Sharon said hastily. "I don't know my financial position, and—"

"I doubt if you have any money," her mother-in-law intervened ruefully. "Rufus was an extravagant boy and didn't leave you well provided for. But that mustn't worry you any more. As I said before, we're your family now and we'll be happy to take care of you."

"I can't let you do that!" Sharon took a step forward. "It isn't that I'm ungrateful—there's nothing I'd like more than to regard you as my family—but I'm young and healthy, apart from having no memory, and I have to make a new life for myself."

"Then make it with us. You're Rufus's widow, and—"

"Adam doesn't like me," Sharon blurted.

"What nonsense! I told you before not to take any notice of his manner. Now you must forget these silly notions of independence and promise to stay here—at least until you've fully recovered."

Sharon half smiled, realising it was childish to argue further. While her past was a blank, it would be wonderful to know she had a home to stay in.

Alone in the bedroom, she allowed the atmosphere to seep into her. How peaceful and gracious everything was! If it were not for Adam's hostility she would like nothing better than to be a part of this lovely place. Yet he so clearly resented her presence, had made so many slighting references to her not being what she seemed, that she knew she would never be at ease with him. She shivered. If only she could remember!

Idly she picked up the photograph of Rufus from the bureau and peered at it. Was this the type of man who attracted her? It must be so, since she had married him, yet she had a feeling she preferred tall, dark men. Immediately she thought of Adam. Her temples began to throb and anxiety took possession of her. It was useless trying to guess the sort of girl she was. She would learn about herself slowly, the way she had learned in the car that she didn't like to smoke.

"But I do prefer dark-haired men," she murmured. "I'm sure of that."

CHAPTER TWO

SHARON was awakened by the sound of a gong. She felt more rested and the return of physical strength brought with it a decrease in the vague forebodings that had filled her earlier.

She washed in the modern bathroom adjoining the bedroom, looking around curiously as she did so. Everything was on a luxurious scale: the sunken bath, the fleecy towels and tablets of expensive, perfumed soap. There was even make-up on the shelf above the wash-basin, and as she applied it, she noticed it was the right shade for a fair-skinned woman. Looking at herself in the mirror was still like looking at a stranger; she moved and gesticulated, watching herself critically as she did so.

The gong sounded again and hurriedly she made for the stairs. She was halfway down when she saw Adam watching her from the hall. In a dinner jacket he looked even more austere, his shirt startlingly white against his dark hair and tanned skin. He waited until she reached the bottom step before he spoke.

"You look better."

"I feel it. I'm not late, am I?"

"This isn't a hotel," he said briefly. "You're at liberty to be late if you wish. We'll go straight into the dining room."

They entered a large, square room with mahogany furniture and a Persian carpet. Sharon glanced at the table and saw it was only set for two.

"Isn't your mother coming down?" she asked.

"No. She has a weak heart and meeting you was a strain."

"I'm sorry."

He shrugged. "At least it's over with. Thank heavens you gave a good performance."

She opened her mouth to protest, then wordlessly took the chair he indicated. They remained silent as Beryl served the meal, and when she had gone, Sharon searched for something to say. But what was the point of making conversation with a man who disliked her? Resolutely she picked up her fork and ate.

The food was delicious and they had reached dessert when she noticed Adam watching her with a strange expression.

"What's the matter?" she asked.

"I'm amazed that you know your likes and dislikes in food, despite having no memory. You enjoy spinach, you declined carrots and peas, and you had two helpings of potato but firmly declined gravy. Now you're displaying a sweet tooth with total disregard for calories."

She looked at her plate, which was piled high with meringue, fruit and whipped cream. "How strange," she exclaimed. "It must be my subconscious. They say that's always a giveaway!"

"You're much too clever to give anything away!"

"Am I? I don't feel particularly clever." She

straightened her shoulders. "But perhaps you know me better than I know myself."

"Perhaps I do."

She bit her lip, determined not to let him bait her into losing her temper.

"Were you happy with Rufus?"

The words were barked out and her fork clattered to the table. Immediately Adam leaned forward and retrieved it.

"I'm sorry," he went on more gently. "I thought I might get more reaction from you if I questioned you abruptly."

"I'd rather you didn't just yet," she said tremulously. "I find you frightening enough as it is, without having you shout at me."

"My God!" It was an explosion of fury. "How can you sound so innocent? You know damn well I could never frighten you!"

"I don't know anything. I keep telling you that." Her voice was trembling, but the look she gave him was steady. "I'm tired of having you treat me as if I'm some kind of criminal. What have I done to make you dislike me?"

"You married Rufus."

"So that's it." There was a pause while she gave careful thought to his statement. "As his older brother, I suppose, you tried to dominate his life and keep him under your thumb?"

"A somewhat distorted view."

"Is it? And is it equally distorted to think he went to South Africa to escape from you?"

Adam went on eating, giving away nothing of his thoughts.

"Did Rufus ask for your permission before he married me?" she continued. "Obviously you didn't give it, or you wouldn't be so rude to me now. But at least your mother didn't object."

"My mother wasn't asked." The words seemed to be forced from him. "Nor did she know the reason Rufus went to Africa."

"What was it?" Adam looked levelly at her. "I suggest we don't continue this conversation. You appear not to remember and I don't want to give you a shock, bearing in mind your request of a moment ago."

"Stop being hypocritical," she snapped. "You'd like nothing better than to shock me. Answer my question and get it over with."

"Very well. But don't say I didn't warn you." He pushed away his plate and leaned back in his chair. "I sent Rufus to South Africa to keep him out of prison."

"Prison!" She clenched her hands. "What had he done?"

"Forged my signature on a cheque, among other things."

"Why?"

"He needed money—rather more than I was prepared to give him. It was to settle a gambling debt. I felt that if he had to sweat it out a bit, it wouldn't do him any harm. I refused to help him and—"

"He forged your name on a cheque."

"Yes. The sum was large and my bank manager rang

me to query it. Rufus and I had a row and I threatened to prosecute him unless he went to South Africa to work."

"Why there?" queried Sharon.

"I believed that on my uncle's farm, in a new country, he might find his feet."

She pondered for a moment. "That still doesn't explain why you dislike me."

"Because you married my brother for what you could get out of him. If you'd loved him you wouldn't have forced him to remain in Cape Town. Nor would you have encouraged him to gamble and drink and write to me every month for money."

Astonishment held her silent. This man couldn't be talking about her. He must be thinking of another woman. She hated gambling and she loathed a man who drank too much. She knew it in her bones, felt it in every cell of her body.

"If you had genuinely cared for Rufus," Adam continued, "you could have helped him to make something of himself! As it was—"

"You're wrong!" She pushed back her chair. "Not about Rufus—I daresay you knew your brother better than I did—but you're wrong about me. I'm not the sort of person you think I am."

"If you like, I can show you some of the letters Rufus wrote to me. They refer to you and your insatiable demands. They—"

"No!" she cried. "It isn't true. It can't be!"

She ran to the door, but before she could open it, it swung forward and a man came in. He was nearly as tall as Adam but heavier in build, with reddish hair and a weatherbeaten face.

"I'm sorry, Adam," he murmured. "I didn't know you had a guest."

"Sharon is family." Adam rose. "Allow me to introduce you. Sharon, this is Simon Lennox, my bailiff."

A large hand engulfed Sharon's. "So you're Rufus's wife—I mean widow."

She smiled faintly, wincing slightly at his heavy grip. He released her hand and stepped aside to let her go out.

"I hope you're not leaving because of me," he said with a grin.

"I was going anyway." For some unaccountable reason she felt the colour suffuse her face and knew he did not close the door of the dining room until she was halfway up the stairs.

At the top of the steps she hesitated, then walked slowly along the hall until she saw light seeping from under a door. She paused again, then knocked softly and entered. Mrs. Peters was sitting up in bed, her dinner tray pushed to one side.

"Why, Sharon, how nice of you to come and see me!" she smiled.

"I wondered if I could get you anything?"

"No, thank you, dear. I'm sorry I couldn't come down to dinner, but I felt too tired. Anyway, it gave you and Adam a chance to get to know each other. I hope he behaved himself?"

"We had an interesting talk," Sharon said evasively.

"Good. In a few days I'm sure you'll begin to understand him and be friends. Now run along to bed, child. You look as pale as a ghost."

"I do feel rather tired," Sharon admitted.

"I'm not surprised. It's your first day out of hospital, and meeting Rufus's family for the first time, too. You'll be better after a night's sleep."

But sleep did not come easily to Sharon and for several hours she pondered everything Adam had said, more than ever determined to leave as soon as she knew where to go and what to do.

Did the airline have her South African address and would she find out more about herself if she went back there? Many possibilities occurred to her, but none were to her liking. According to Adam she had come to England to better herself financially from the Peters family, and though she found this alien to her way of thinking, she had to stay until some other kind of truth emerged.

With this thought she fell into an uneasy slumber, only awakening as a sunbeam filtered through a chink in the curtains and slanted across her eyes. She reached for her watch, then flung aside the bedclothes.

A clock was delicately chiming nine in the distance as she descended the stairs and saw Beryl entering through a green baize door.

"Good morning, Mrs. Rufus. I didn't know you were coming down for breakfast. The master left instructions not to disturb you."

"Doesn't anyone come down for it?" asked Sharon.

"Only Mr. Adam. He always has breakfast in the sun parlour."

Following the girl along a narrow passage behind the stairs, Sharon found herself in a glass-covered porch. She stopped in dismay as she saw Adam seated at a round table, a newspaper in one hand, a piece of toast in the other. This morning he wore jodhpurs and a polo-necked sweater. Its colour—bright canary yellow—accentuated his dark good looks.

"Good morning, Sharon." He stood and indicated the chair opposite him. "The toast and coffee are still hot, but if you'd like anything else, Beryl will get it for you."

"I never eat a big breakfast," she said, and stopped, flushing as she saw the fine crescents of his eyebrows lift. "Little bits of information come back like that," she explained.

He nodded and resumed his seat but remained silent till Beryl had departed. "Thank you for going in to see Mother last night. She appreciates small courtesies."

"She deserves them. She's very kind."

"Too kind," he said hardly. "She's always helping some lame duck or another—usually females who take advantage of her."

Sharon buttered some toast. "You don't like women, do you?"

"I don't dislike them."

"But you aren't married?" As he shook his head Sharon noticed he was looking beyond her to a slim figure on horseback barely visible through a clump of trees.

"Helen's just arriving," he said, rising to his feet. "If

you'll excuse me." On the threshold he paused. "Have you made any plans for today?"

"Your mother said something about us going to London. I need some clothes and—" Sharon nibbled her lip, embarrassed and reluctant to talk money with him. Yet she would have to do so sooner or later, and the longer she put it off, the more difficult it would become. "I don't want to buy anything until I know what I can afford. I don't even know if I have a bank account!"

"You have no cause for alarm." Adam's voice was cold. "You'll get compensation from the airline, but in any event you're my responsibility now."

"I don't want to be!"

"Really? You may be suffering from amnesia, but it would take more than a blow on the head to alter your character!"

Before she could think of a suitable retort, he walked out.

Sharon's appetite went with him and she flung down her napkin. How dared he talk to her as if she were a gold-digger? But maybe she was. After all, she had apparently encouraged Rufus in his gambling and had instigated the begging letters he had written to his brother.

"I don't believe it!" she cried.

"Don't believe what?"

Swinging around, she saw Simon Lennox behind her. "I—I was thinking aloud," she stammered. "I didn't know anyone was here."

"I hope I'm not intruding?"

She shook her head. "Did you want to see Adam?"

"I'd rather see you." His smile was warm. "Actually, I did come to see Adam, but I spotted him riding off with Helen, so I thought I'd drop in and say hello. Mind if I sit down?" He did so without waiting for her assent. "There wouldn't be any coffee going, would there?"

She nodded and poured him a cup, aware of his eyes on her as she did so.

"You're not the way I imagined," he said.

"How did you imagine me?"

"More sophisticated. And I never thought you'd be half as lovely as you are."

"Thank you." Her tone was so dry he looked at her reproachfully.

"I mean it. I don't give idle compliments, Mrs. Peters. One of my assets—or failings, depending on which way you look at it—is that I always say what I think."

"At the moment I'd regard that as an asset," she replied.

"Good. Then I hope we can be friends?"

He helped himself to sugar and she asked idly, "Who's Helen?"

"Helen Ferrer. She's your nearest neighbour. She lives at Tower Lodge and she and Adam have known each other since they were children."

"They must have a lot in common," she observed.

"Horses, chiefly. By the way, do you ride?"

"I've no idea." She smiled at his look of astonishment. "I've lost my memory, Mr. Lennox."

"Of course, I was forgetting. It must be damned awkward for you!"

"It is. Still, I'm gradually learning about myself: I like spinach, I don't like carrots, and I'm almost sure I don't smoke."

He laughed. "We must put your riding capabilities to the test some time." Pushing back his chair, he gave a brief salute, walked over the balustrade and set off down the garden.

Sharon watched him go with regret, contrasting his cordial manner with Adam's sombre one. Apart from which, his obvious admiration was a much-needed boost to her self-confidence.

"Excuse me, Mrs. Rufus," Beryl spoke from behind. "Madam wondered if you would go up and see her when you've finished breakfast."

"I'll go right away."

Mrs. Peters was dressed and sitting by her desk when Sharon entered her warm, flower-filled room.

"Good morning, my dear. I hope you're looking forward to our outing?"

"I will be if I know I can repay what you spend on me when the airline pays me compensation."

"What a foolish thing to be worrying about! You're the girl Rufus married and it's my duty—my pleasure—to take care of you."

"It's kind of you to say that, but—"

"No, no. I don't want to talk about it any more."

Mrs. Peters's heightened colour dissuaded Sharon from further argument, and watching her mother-in-law's face as they sat in Paul Duval's salon later that morning, she knew that any discussion about money would have to take place with Adam.

"We must have at least half a dozen outfits to take with us," Mrs. Peters informed the couturier. "The poor child has absolutely nothing to wear."

"Then I suggest you choose some clothes from our boutique. The couture ones require two or three fittings for every garment."

"The boutique sounds much more my line," Sharon said at once.

"But the clothes I've earmarked from the collection are so lovely," Mrs. Peters protested.

"I'm sure the boutique ones are just as lovely."

Determinedly Sharon headed for the ground floor, where she was joined by her mother-in-law who, seeing the rows of delectable garments, all with Monsieur Duval's individual stamp of creativity, promptly ordered three times as many as before, so that the money spent equalled the original amount.

"Monsieur Duval must regard you as one of his best clients," Sharon remarked as they finally drove away. She had happily discarded the dress she had set out in and was now wearing a Duval two-piece in sheer wool.

"I enjoy spending money," Mrs. Peters rejoined. "My father was a Yorkshire textile magnate, and you know the Yorkshire saying, don't you?"

"I'm afraid not."

"Money is like manure—it does best when it's spread around!"

Sharon laughed. "Is looking after lame ducks part of your spreading it around?"

"I can see Adam's been talking to you. He's always trying to show me that the people I help are only out to use me."

"Aren't they?" asked Sharon.

"Some are. But it doesn't bother me."

The woman peered through the window and Sharon saw they had stopped outside a hairdressing salon.

"If you feel up to it," Mrs. Peters suggested, "I'd like Gerald to do your hair. Now he's a lame duck who actually turned into a swan!"

Full of curiosity, Sharon entered the crowded salon. A wavy-haired young man rushed forward to greet Mrs. Peters as though she were his mother. Fairy godmother, Sharon decided, learning from the conversation that her mother-in-law had given him the money to open his own establishment.

"I want you to work your magic on my daughter-in-law," Mrs. Peters informed him. "I hope you can fit her in?"

"For you I can do anything," Gerald said grandiloquently, and gave Sharon's hair a piercing appraisal. "It's frightfully out of condition, you know. Another week and it would start falling out!"

"Then I've just got here in time," she said, straight-faced, and followed him to a cubicle.

Late-afternoon traffic was clogging the West End when the chauffeur-driven Bentley headed for the West Country. Sharon felt like a doll that had been made over, in her new clothes and with her hair cut slightly and gleaming like platinum as it lay smooth over her head to show off her well-shaped crown and the nape of her delicate neck.

"I thought you were lovely the moment I saw you," Mrs. Peters commented, "but I'd no idea you were quite so beautiful."

"Fine feathers make fine birds," Sharon smiled.

"It's more than feathers, my dear. You've a natural radiance. I can see why Rufus adored you."

Mention of Rufus dimmed Sharon's pleasure in the moment and she huddled back in her seat, twisting her wedding ring round and round her finger. She could imagine Adam's scathing look when he saw her in her newly acquired finery and wished she could turn tail and run. But run where? And to whom?

It was six-thirty when they arrived home and Mrs. Peters announced that she was going to rest before dinner.

"Why not have dinner in your room?" Sharon suggested. "I'll join you there, if you like. It's been a long day for you."

"I want you to dine with Adam. I can't wait for him to see you. Put on the blue dress. It's the one I like best."

"A lovely creation to be worn by a lovely creation." Sharon could not contain an upsurge of frustration. "Without any memory and with these new clothes and hairstyle I feel as if I've been manufactured!"

"My poor child!" Mrs Peters clasped her close. "Perhaps it won't be so miserable for you if you try to think you've been manufactured for me. For years I waited for my sons to marry and give me daughters, and when Rufus did—but remained in Africa—I was heartbroken. But now you're here and—" The soft voice died away and the woman moved to the stairs.

"Mrs. Peters!" Sharon ran after her and caught her hand as it rested on the banister. "Thank you for saying that. You've made me feel as if I belong somewhere."

CHAPTER THREE

SHARON walked down the stairs, self-conscious in the deceptively simple dress of sapphire blue velvet that skimmed her body like the tender hands of a lover. Instinctively she knew she had never before worn a dress as expensive as this, nor used as much make-up as that supplied by the beautician who had been another of Mrs. Peters's finds. Brown mascara accentuated her long, curling lashes and a glowing foundation hid the pallor caused by her accident.

At least make-up gave one a mask to don, she decided, as she took a deep breath, pushed open the drawing-room door and walked in.

Two figures standing close together in front of the fireplace drew swiftly apart. Sharon stopped short and Adam's pale grey eyes narrowed at the sight of her. But he said nothing and turned to the woman at his side.

"Helen, I'd like you to meet my sister-in-law, Sharon, this is Helen Ferrer; a good friend and close neighbour."

Sharon held out her hand and felt it taken in a firm, almost masculine grasp. Helen Ferrer was in her late twenties, almost as tall as Adam, her hair the same blue-black. She had small, symmetrical features redeemed from coldness by a wide, slightly artificial smile that showed neat, foxish teeth.

"So we meet at last." Her voice, like her appearance,

was as cool as a mountain stream. "I can see why Adam was surprised."

"I seem to surprise a great many people," Sharon remarked as she sank down on a pouffe in front of the fire. "It's difficult trying to be someone I don't remember."

"I wouldn't worry about it. You'll probably do just as well, if not better, without recollecting the past. I wish I could forget the past few years."

"It would help if you'd look to the future," Adam said gently.

"I'm already doing that, with your help."

Helen's expression was so intimate that Sharon looked away. Then she heard Adam move to the sideboard.

"What will you have to drink, Sharon?"

"I don't drink spirits."

"Since when? Rufus said you were a great gin drinker."

"Am I?" She was surprised. "A great gin drinker" seemed an uninspiring thing to be. "I don't know why I refused. The words just popped out."

"Then you'll have one?"

She nodded and accepted a narrow tumbler from him. Cautiously she sipped, shuddered and held out the glass. "Not for me, thanks. It's awful!"

Adam took the glass. "Maybe the plane crash affected your taste buds."

"It must have." She moved closer to the fire. "It's very cold here."

Helen laughed. "We're supposed to be having a warm spring. What will you say in the winter?"

"Sharon won't be here in the winter," Adam intervened. "She's only staying a month."

Sharon fixed him with a cold stare. "Am I?"

"That's what we agreed before you came."

"Agreed what?" a thin voice enquired, and they all turned to see Mrs. Peters by the door.

"Sharon came over only for a month," Adam said steadily.

"I'm sure she'll stay longer if we make her feel welcome. A month is far too short to get properly acquainted." The old lady smiled at Helen. "What do you think of my daughter-in-law?"

"That's a leading question to ask in front of me!" Sharon interposed.

"She hasn't been here long enough, either," Helen Ferrer said waspishly. "One can't form a judgment in a few hours."

"I can." Mrs. Peters settled on the couch and regarded her daughter-in-law. "I feel as though I've known you for years. I wish Rufus could see how beautiful you are tonight."

There was an uncomfortable silence, broken at last by Helen speaking to Adam.

"I saw Simon coming out of the Bull this afternoon. He seems to spend most of his spare time there. I don't know why you keep him."

"Because he's efficient," Adam replied shortly. "What he does in his own time is not my concern."

"Maybe not. But you should warn Sharon that he has an eye for the ladies."

"I've already met him," Sharon said, "and I found him charming."

"He meant you to! Charm is his stock in trade."

"He's coming over for coffee this evening," Adam interrupted, "so I suggest we drop the subject." He put out his arm to his mother. "Let's go in to dinner. I'm not going to let you take advantage of Sharon's presence by staying up late."

"What a bully you are!" his mother pouted.

"But you love it!"

His smile was the warmest Sharon had seen him display as he bent to help his mother to her feet.

Conversation at dinner centred on people Sharon didn't know. Mrs. Peters tried to steer it towards general topics, but Helen kept returning to the more intimate, "Do you remember?" Looking at the dark-haired girl, Sharon wondered what had prompted her remarks about the bailiff. Even it what she had said was true, it would have been less malicious to have kept quiet.

When dinner was over, they retired to the drawing-room. Sharon once more took her place by the fire and watched with mingled amusement and antipathy as Helen poured the coffee. She invested the simple task with a majesty that increased Sharon's dislike of her. It was obvious the woman saw herself as the future mistress of Green Spinney and, looking at Adam's dark countenance, she wondered if Helen was already *his*.

"Your coffee, Sharon." She saw him approaching her, a cup in his hand. His eyes rested momentarily on the curve of her breasts and she hastily straightened.

"The firelight is turning your hair to pure silver,"

Mrs. Peters said suddenly. "It's easy to see what you'll look like when you're an old lady."

"What a depressing thought!" Helen commented. "As a brunette I'm dreading going through the pepper-and-salt stage. Is your hair natural, Sharon?"

"I don't know."

"Don't be silly!" Mrs. Peters expostulated. "Gerald said he had never seen such a glorious natural colour."

Adam's hand jerked and his coffee cup fell to the floor and shattered.

"Damn!" He bent to pick up the pieces and dab the liquid with his handkerchief. "I hope I haven't stained your dress, Sharon?"

"I don't think so."

"How clumsy of you, Adam!" Mrs. Peters scolded.

"I know."

He kept his face averted as he went on dabbing at the carpet.

At that moment Simon Lennox came in. He greeted Mrs. Peters and Helen, then turned to Sharon and did an undisguised doubletake.

"Good lord! I hardly recognised you."

"How unflattering! Was I a monster before or after?"

"Neither. This morning you were great and this evening you're greater!" Accepting a cup of coffee from Adam, he took a chair between Sharon and her mother-in-law. "Have you thought any more about riding with me? There's nothing better for keeping you fit."

"I'm still not sure I *can* ride," said Sharon. "I don't remember."

"I shouldn't think it likely," Helen said.

"Why do you say that?"

"You don't seem the type."

Sharon bit back an angry retort, convinced Helen was deliberately being rude.

"We can soon find out," Simon interposed cheerily. "I have to ride over to the Rockforth farm tomorrow and Mrs. Rufus can come with me."

Sharon glanced at Adam, but he was pouring himself another cup of coffee.

"Thank you," she said slowly. "I'd like that." She stood up. "I think I'll take a stroll in the garden. Being with a lot of people makes me feel a bit on edge."

"Would you like Adam to go with you?" Mrs. Peters asked.

"I'll be fine on my own."

Picking up a coat from the hall, Sharon slung it around her shoulders and walked down the drive. A cool wind blew through her hair and she heaved a sigh of relief. It was good to be alone. The evening had exhausted her and the conversation, with its undercurrent of latent hostility—at least on the part of Adam and Helen—had filled her with futile anger. If only she could remember! Although convinced she was not like the woman Adam believed her to be, she was powerless to disprove his accusations until her memory returned.

Deep in thought, she didn't realise she wasn't alone until she turned and saw Simon.

"I'm just leaving," he said. "You'd better go in. Mrs. Peters is worried about you."

"I'll go right away," she told him.

"Don't forget our date tomorrow."

"I won't." She stopped short. "Oh dear, I won't be able to make it after all. I haven't any riding kit, not even a pair of slacks."

He looked at her in dismay, then slapped his thigh. "I've a pair of my sister's jodhpurs at my place. She left them last time she came down. I'm sure they'll fit you. I'll bring them over first thing in the morning."

"Please don't go to all that trouble. We can ride some other time."

"It's no trouble. Anyway, I'm looking forward to our outing."

With a cheery salute he went down the drive and Sharon returned to the house. Whether or not Helen's remarks about his being a flirt were true, it was impossible not to like him.

Though reluctant to see Adam and Helen, she was unwilling to go to bed without saying good night to her mother-in-law, and drawing a deep breath, she entered the drawing room. Helen was there alone, but before Sharon could step back out, the girl beckoned her in.

"Adam's taken his mother to her room. Come in and keep me company. Did you see Simon in the garden?"

"For a moment."

Helen's mocking glance made words unnecessary and Sharon felt herself colouring.

"I think I'll go to bed myself. I'm rather tired."

"Don't rush off yet. This is a good opportunity for us to get acquainted."

Sharon shrugged and sat down.

"Do you think you'll stay here the month?" Helen asked.

"I don't see why not."

"I'd hate to stay anywhere I wasn't welcome." The dark eyes sparkled angrily. "You must know what Adam thinks of you!"

"I know what he thought of his brother! And I think he behaved without any understanding!"

"He did the only thing he could. His main desire was to keep his mother ignorant of what a swine Rufus was!"

"Obviously you didn't like Rufus, either!"

"I loathed him!" said Helen vehemently.

"Why?"

"You can ask me that?" Helen glared at her. "Don't you know that before he went to Africa I was going to marry him?"

"No." Sharon absorbed the knowledge but couldn't feel any emotion about it. "Or at least if I did know, I can't remember."

Helen snorted. "You'll be telling me next you don't know about the cheque and the jewellery?"

"I'm afraid I don't." Sharon moistened her lips. "At least, I—Adam only told me about the cheque."

"Rufus stole some jewellery, too—from his mother. Adam will give you the details if you don't believe me. Mrs. Peters doesn't know, of course. Adam let her think it was a burglar." Helen crossed one slim leg over the other. "He told me, though. He hoped I could make Rufus return it, but unfortunately it didn't work out that way. Rufus had already sold the stuff."

"What happened after that?" asked Sharon.

"I broke my engagement. Adam was furious. He had

wanted me to marry Rufus and go away with him. It's only in the last few months that he's come round to my way of thinking." Helen's eyes narrowed. "He realises no decent girl could have stayed with him; he was an out-and-out rotter!"

Sharon sprang up. "You're being very insulting."

"I don't mean to be. I thought we were talking straight."

"Straight venom," Sharon retorted, and stalked angrily from the room.

By the time she was outside her mother-in-law's bedroom she had managed to control her temper, and she looked unruffled as she entered and paused by the bed.

"I'm sorry I stayed out so long," she apologized. "I got lost in thought and didn't realise how late it was."

"Not sad thoughts, I hope?"

"Oh, no." Impulsively Sharon bent and kissed the lined cheek. "I couldn't be sad when you're so good to me."

"I haven't even started yet. You're going to be so happy here, you'll never want to leave." The older woman patted her hand. "I'm glad you're going riding with Simon."

"I nearly cried off," Sharon admitted. "I don't have any riding clothes, but he's lending me a pair of his sister's trousers."

"I never knew he had a sister." Mrs. Peters yawned and Sharon retreated to the door. "Come and see me in the morning, child."

"I will. And thank you again for everything."

In her own room, Sharon undressed and sat by the

window, too restless to sleep. Everything she had learned from Helen returned to haunt her, making her wonder how she could have married a man so devoid of principles. Helen had said Rufus had charm, but she could not see herself being so carried away by that trait that she would lose her sense of judgment. She pressed her hands to her temples. Had she loved Rufus so blindly that she hadn't seen him for what he was? Or was she, as Adam maintained, no better than Rufus had been?

She jumped up and crossed to the bureau. She gazed intently at the photograph of her husband, willing herself to remember.

The sound of a car moving down the drive brought her back to the present. Adam must be taking Helen home. She glanced at her watch. It was midnight. She thought of the dinner she had left almost untouched and the breakfast that was still eight hours away. She debated what to do about the hunger that now gnawed at her. Deciding that if she remained hungry she would never get to sleep, she slipped on the full-skirted red dressing gown that lay at the foot of the bed—another present acquired that day—and tiptoed down the stairs.

All the lights were out except a small lamp on the hall table. Her foot was on the bottom step when the library door was flung open, and she half screamed, suppressing it as she recognized Adam.

"I thought you were a burglar! I heard a car leave and—"

"Helen drove herself home." He moved nearer, though his face was still in shadow. "What do you want?"

"Some milk and munch."

"What?"

"I'm hungry," Sharon explained. "I didn't have much dinner—I was too nervous."

"Or too excited by the loot you'd acquired!" He paused as though expecting her angry denial.

"I'm not going to let you bait me, Adam. I can't defend myself when I don't know myself."

"You know how you feel," he said coldly.

"I only know I feel so different from—oh, what's the use!" Sharon flung away to the door that led to the kitchen quarters and then, halfway through it, stopped and turned. "Helen told me that Rufus stole some of his mother's jewellery. I'm positive I didn't know about it."

"Perhaps my brother didn't tell you. There may be many things you don't know about him." Adam strode over to her. "How real is your amnesia, I wonder? You look like an angel with your big blue eyes and silver-gilt hair, yet I know that underneath you're—" Sombrely he allowed his eyes to speak the words he would not say, his gaze roving her body with slow intensity.

"Why do you hate me so much?" she asked. "What have I done to you?"

"It's what you're doing," he said thickly, catching her abruptly by the shoulders. "Such innocence!" he muttered, peering into her face. "What are you like behind the angel mask?"

Any reply she might have made was stifled as his mouth came down on hers. She stiffened with resistance, but he ignored it, his lips increasing their pressure until they forced her own to part. The heat from him seemed to intensify, melting her anger and dissolving her fear.

Her arms clasped his neck and she relaxed against him, her senses telling her she was travelling a road she had never travelled before. But desire showed her the way, propelled her hands to his hair, his back, beneath his jacket to his chest. His thighs were like steel against her own, his muscles riding as passion began to overcome control.

As suddenly as he had caught her, he let her go and she swayed against the wall.

"Adam—"

"No!" Without another word he turned on his heel and left her.

CHAPTER FOUR

SHARON could not face the prospect of seeing Adam the next morning and decided to have breakfast with Mrs. Peters.

She was coming out of the bathroom when Beryl entered with a parcel containing a pair of jodhpurs and a riding jacket.

"They're from Mr. Lennox. He said to tell you he'll be waiting for you at ten."

"I only hope they fit," Sharon smiled, and proceeded to put them on.

Regarding her reflection a little later she was delighted with her appearance. Simon's sister was near enough her own size to give an idea of how well a perfectly tailored riding outfit would suit her. If she stayed here for any length of time she would have one made. The idea brought with it the knowledge that she was a guest on sufferance, and her pleasure in the morning ahead dimmed.

But her smile was bright as she entered Mrs. Peters's room and found her sitting up in bed, surrounded by pastel-coloured cushions.

"You look good in trousers, my dear. I can just picture you on a horse."

"I only hope I can stay on it long enough to justify the bother!" smiled Sharon. "I must say these things feel familiar to me, though. I'm sure I've worn jodhpurs before."

She pivoted and then perched on the bed as Mrs Peters' personal maid, a grey-haired, thin-faced woman called Margaret, wheeled in a trolley with two breakfasts set out on it.

Between sipping coffee and eating toast, Sharon read aloud titbits of gossip from a couple of newspapers and Mrs. Peters capped several anecdotes with others of her own. Sharon could easily imagine her as a young girl waltzing her way through London society, leaving a trail of broken hearts.

"Do you enjoy living in the country?" Sharon asked. "I'd have thought it rather dull if you're restricted in what you do."

"I can still go for drives and enjoy the garden. Besides, I'm not young, like you. I need peace and quiet."

"So do I," Sharon said with heartfelt agreement.

"I'm sure you won't when you're completely better. I wish you'd stay here permanently."

"I can't." Sharon visualised Adam's reaction to his mother's remark. "In fact, I'd like to leave quite soon."

"But you've only just arrived! And we've so much to talk about. I'm hoping that when your memory returns we'll be able to talk about Rufus." The lined face puckered. "Aren't you happy here? I know I can be a bossy old lady, but—"

"That's not true!" Sharon sank on her knees beside the bed. "You've been marvellous to me. Warm and kind and generous. I feel as if I've known you all my life. In fact, I *have* known you all the life I can remember!"

"Then why must you talk of leaving? Has Adam said something to upset you?"

"It has nothing to do with him."

"I can easily talk to him and—"

"No! Please don't!" Sharon begged anxiously.

"Then why the sudden urge to go? Is it because of Helen?"

"I couldn't care less about Helen."

"Ah! She *did* say something to upset you!" Mrs. Peters looked pleased with her guesswork. "I suppose Rufus didn't tell you he'd been engaged to her? He always hated admitting he'd done anything he regretted. As a little boy he'd get furious if he was caught doing something naughty. Quite different from Adam, in that respect. He'd always own up. Sometimes he even took the blame for Rufus. I always knew, mind you, though I pretended I didn't." Mrs. Peters pursed her lips. "But where was I? Oh yes—Helen."

"My wanting to go has nothing to do with her," Sharon stated. "I swear it."

"I'm glad. She's had a very unhappy life. She was so upset when Rufus went to South Africa that she left the district and married a man years older than herself. When he died she came back here and has tried to rebuild her life."

"She seems to be doing quite well," Sharon replied, "though suffering doesn't seem to have taught her compassion."

"We don't all learn by our experiences," Mrs. Peters murmured. "Helen's a nice girl but a trifle hard. I'm telling you this so you won't mind her sharp tongue.

This is your home now, Sharon. Nothing can alter that."

"Except Helen's marriage to Adam!"

There was a long pause, broken only by Mrs. Peters pushing the trolley away from the bed.

"I shouldn't have said that," Sharon apologised. "It's only natural for you to want him to marry. And if he and Helen—"

"There's nothing between them, officially," said Mrs. Peters. "Adam sees quite a bit of her, but he's never spoken to me about his feelings for her. That's a sure sign he isn't certain about them. But even if he does marry her, your home is still with me. We can both move to another house, maybe a rustic cottage somewhere nearby."

Tears blurred Sharon's vision and she almost wished Adam would marry Helen at once. Then the cottage could become a reality and she would have no need to go away.

"Please stay," Mrs. Peters repeated. "You agreed to a month—I heard Adam say so. If you want to leave after that, I won't argue with you."

It was impossible to refuse such a request, and Sharon nodded.

"I feel as if I've known you far longer than a couple of days," Mrs. Peters went on. "You're exactly the wife I'd have chosen for Rufus—for either of my sons, in fact."

Sharon tried to see herself as Adam's wife and quickly shied away from the thought. "You still miss Rufus terribly, don't you?" she asked.

"Yes. The year he left home was dreadful for me. Everything went wrong. I lost some of my favourite pieces of jewellery—to this day we've never discovered who stole them—and Adam went around in the blackest mood I've ever seen him in. For months after Rufus left he was barely civil to anyone. They were very fond of each other, you know."

"I can't imagine Adam being fond of anybody," Sharon commented.

"That's because you don't understand him. He feels things very deeply and he's reluctant to let people know it." Blue-veined hands plucked at the sheet. "I don't know why he's so rude to you. I'm sure it has something to do with his attachment to Rufus."

"I'm sure you're right." Sharon clutched at this suggestion like a drowning man at a straw. Far better for Mrs. Peters to think this than to guess that Adam considered his sister-in-law a gold-digger and an unloving wife to his brother. "I'm sure my being here reminds him of things he wants to forget. It will be better for him when I leave."

"But I don't want you to leave! I'll talk to him and—"

"No!" Sharon put her hand over her mother-in-law's. "I agreed to stay a month and I will. Now please don't get excited. It's bad for you." She gently pushed the trembling body back against the cushions. "If you'll tell me where your pills are—"

"I don't need my pills." Mrs. Peters closed her eyes. "It's this ridiculous heart of mine. The doctor's always warning me not to get excited. That's why you mustn't talk of leaving."

Sharon could not help smiling. Less than sixty seconds ago her mother-in-law had agreed not to press her to stay more than a month; now it was turning into forever. "Dear mama-in-law, you're trying to blackmail me!"

"I know!" The faded eyes were bright with unexpected mischief. "And I hope I'm going to win. Now run along or you'll be late for your date with Simon."

Thankfully Sharon went down to the garden. Heartwarming though her mother-in-law's admiration for her was, it nevertheless imposed an obligation on her she was reluctant to fulfil. Slowly she made her way to the stables, brushing aside her problems when she saw Simon Lennox.

"I'm glad to see the clothes fit you," he smiled.

"Perfectly." She watched as he led out two horses. "Which one's mine?"

He indicated a glossy chestnut mare and Sharon stroked the velvety nose.

"What a beauty you are! Even if I find I can't ride, it's going to be a pleasure to fall off you!"

But no sooner was she in the saddle than she knew she was a capable horsewoman, and to prove it, she dug in her knees and gave the animal its head.

She had galloped a mile across country before Simon caught up with her. She reined in and turned to him, laughing, as he drew abreast. Then they trotted side by side.

"You can certainly ride!" he exclaimed.

"It was wonderful! How far is it to the Rockforth farm?"

"We'll be there in ten minutes. My business won't take long."

"I don't mind. I'll take a stroll while I'm waiting. It's time I saw something of the countryside."

It was ten-thirty when they reached the farmhouse and, leaving Simon to tether their horses, Sharon wandered off to explore. Climbing a stile, she crossed a field and entered a small wood where tall saplings sheltered clumps of crocuses, daffodils and vivid patches of moss. Walking down a slope she came to a clear stream rippling over shiny pebbles. She sat on the bank and idly threw stones into the water. A fish moved beneath the surface and a large bubble formed on the water. She drew a deep breath. How peaceful it was here! If only she need never go back to the dark house with its hostile master.

Thoughts of Adam brought even more unpleasant thoughts. Was he right in his assessment of her or were her own instincts about herself more reliable? Although she longed for her memory to return, she dreaded it, afraid there might be truth in the accusations he had hurled at her.

Twigs crackled and she turned to see Simon approaching. His hair blew in the breeze and the yellow silk kerchief around his throat made a patch of colour beneath his tanned face.

Sharon glanced at her watch. "I'm sorry, I didn't realise I'd been here so long."

"It's no sweat. I was through sooner than I expected, so I thought I'd come and look for you." He flopped on the bank at her feet. "It was a bit of luck for me, your coming to Green Spinney. There aren't any attractive girls round these parts."

"What about Helen?"

"Too hard-boiled for my liking." He leaned on his elbow and stared at her. "I hope you're going to like it here."

"I love it," she said, then changed the subject. "Does your sister come down often?"

"No. She lives in London."

"Is she younger than you?"

"Yes."

"What does she do?"

A withdrawn look came over his face. "She's always changing jobs and I can never keep track of her."

"Well, I'm glad you kept track of her long enough for her to come down and leave her riding kit here."

Before she could move Simon stretched out his arm and pulled her forward until his lips could press hers in a moist and demanding kiss. Instantly she pushed him away and jumped to her feet.

"You had no right to do that!" she exclaimed angrily.

He scrambled up, his expression rueful. "It's your own fault. You shouldn't look so kissable."

"I've no intention of walking round wearing a yashmak!" Sharon was only partly mollified. "I don't like being kissed by strangers."

"I won't do it again, unless I'm asked." He stretched out his hand. "Forgiven?"

She shrugged and set off the way they had come. The tranquillity of the wood calmed her, helping her to put the scene with Simon into perspective. It was childish to flare up over a kiss—anyone would think she was an untouched virgin! Yet her body had recoiled from the open passion Simon Lennox had displayed, though the previous night— She mused on this, trying and failing to find some clue about herself in the way she had reacted.

"You will see me again, won't you?" he asked.

"Why not?" Her composure was restored. "I enjoy riding with you."

It was still half an hour before lunch when she returned to Green Spinney, and after she had changed she wandered into the library. Of all the rooms she had seen here, she liked this one the best. It was semi-circular, with a wide bay window jutting out on to a little terrace of its own.

The decor of the room was definitely masculine. The carpet was dark blue and wine, the drapes of wine silk and the armchairs covered with a cinnamon-coloured leather. A great rosewood desk stood in the window bay, its top pristine; even the nibs of the old-fashioned pens were clean and shiny. Somehow she knew this room had never belonged to Rufus: everything about it was redolent of Adam.

A pipe lay on the mantelpiece and she curved her hand around the bowl. She imagined the stem between his lips and unwillingly remembered his kiss. There had been no love in it; only passion and contempt.

"What are you doing in here?"

Startled, she swung around. The pipe fell from her hand and broke on the marble hearth.

Angrily Adam strode forward. "Why were you holding my pipe?" he demanded.

"I—I—" Mortified, she knelt to pick up the pieces.

"Leave them," he commanded. "I'll do it."

She rose. "I'm awfully sorry, but you frightened me."

"You shouldn't have been in here. This room is private."

Annoyed by his tone, her contrition vanished. "Must you be so rude? I should have thought good manners were the first things your mother taught you."

"When I look at you I'm inclined to forget what my mother taught me." His eyes lingered on her mouth before travelling down the slender line of her body. "I'm also beginning to understand what Rufus saw in you."

"I'm sure you don't mean that as a compliment," she said coldly.

"Take it how you like. You know yourself better than I do."

"But I don't." Childishly she rubbed her knuckles into her eyes. "I don't know myself at all—that's the trouble."

Negligently Adam leaned against the mantelpiece. The pose pulled the material of his tight-fitting slacks and outlined his muscular thighs.

"I'll play your game a little longer, Sharon. What would you like to know about yourself? I'll do my best to enlighten you."

She decided to ignore his sarcasm and accept his offer at face value. "What happened between Rufus and Helen?" she asked

"I thought Helen told you."

"Not all of it. Why were you angry with her for not going to South Africa with him?"

"I thought you wanted to find out about yourself," he said, "not about me."

"If you answer my question it will help me to at least understand what Rufus was like."

Adam half turned away, giving her a view of his clean-cut profile. "He was weak and gullible. That's why I wanted Helen to go with him—she had the strength of character he lacked. Unfortunately she didn't have the courage."

"Or maybe the love." There was silence. "You must love a man very much to be willing to marry him and try to reform him."

"Don't make me believe you wanted to do that!"

Resolutely she held on to her temper. "Your mother has no idea what Rufus did, has she?"

"No—and she must never find out. The shock could kill her. She still thinks of him the way he used to be as a youngster."

"Was it fair to keep her in ignorance? Fair to yourself, I mean? I'm sure she feels you could have persuaded him not to go to South Africa."

"I don't mind how harsh my mother thinks me. Rufus was her favourite and I'll protect her memory of him if it's the last thing I do. That's why I didn't want you to come here, why I pretended not to know your whereabouts after he died. Then like a fool I left one of your letters on my desk—luckily only the envelope, so she didn't read the charming contents. But she found your address on the back of it and wrote inviting you to come here for a holiday, all expenses paid."

"Is that why you're so furious with me? Because I came?"

"Does it surprise you?" he said savagely. "Especially when I'd already paid you five thousand pounds—with the promise of a regular allowance—to stay away!"

"You *what*?" Sharon recoiled from the words as if they were poisoned darts.

"You heard me. Five thousand pounds *and* an allowance. But when you received my mother's invitation you wired back and said you were on your way."

Sharon listened to what she had done as if she were hearing the action of a stranger. Yet they *were* the actions of a stranger; for the more unpleasant the things Adam accused her of, the less she could credit herself with doing them.

"You make me sound dreadful," she said candidly. "But then your behaviour hasn't been very commendable, either. Your resentment seems to boil down to cash, doesn't it? Are you worried that your mother will leave me something in her will?"

His face darkened with fury, but with a great effort he restrained his temper and moved away from her.

"I have more than enough money of my own. My concern has always been for my mother's peace of mind. I never wanted her to find out the sort of woman Rufus had married."

"Was it so dreadful of me not to want to live on your uncle's farm? Lots of girls would hate that sort of life."

Silently Adam moved to his desk, unlocked a drawer and withdrew a letter.

"Rufus wrote this the week before he was killed. Perhaps you'd like me to read some of it?"

Sharon nodded and, as if afraid of what was coming, sank on to the nearest chair. Adam began to read, his voice harsh in the quiet room.

"I thought Sharon was strong enough to help me overcome my weaknesses—heaven knows I have plenty—but her strength seems to be turned against me and I can't fight it. In the past few days I've thought a lot about Green Spinney and Mother. I've got some bug in my bloodstream and it's making me feel low, hence my sudden attack of honesty! But somehow there doesn't seem much to live for. Sharon will leave me if you don't send me some money. She's found some Argentinian boy-friend and is threatening to run off with him. If you could send me a couple of hundred pounds—"

Adam looked up. "Does that help you to understand why I don't like you?"

Sharon was at a loss for an answer. On the face of it—and she had no reason to think Adam had made up any part of the letter—she was as despicable as he had said. Yet deep in her bones she could not believe she would ever act the way Rufus's wife had done. But she *was* his wife—or at least his widow—which was why she was here.

"Don't tell me you're speechless?" Adam said sarcastically.

"I am," she confessed. "I can't believe I drank heavily and was unfaithful. It doesn't seem like me."

"Doesn't it? I can't say I'm convinced of your good nature, though you've put on a good act."

"You don't want to be convinced. You'll never believe your brother was his own worst enemy. You'd rather put the blame on me." She clutched at the folds of her dress. "Yet you've obviously forgiven Helen for letting him down."

"I forgave her when I realised she wasn't the right woman for him."

"Is she the right woman for you?" Sharon asked coolly, but Adam ignored her and went on speaking.

"When Rufus went to Africa, Helen married on the rebound. It was unhappy from the word go. But when her husband became ill she nursed him devotedly until he died."

"An ideal wife!"

"You may joke about it, but I happen to think it's true." He inclined his head towards the door. "There's no point continuing this conversation. Simon will be here any moment, so perhaps you'd like to go to the drawing room."

"Aren't you afraid I might tell your mother the whole story?" Sharon asked sarcastically.

"I'd strangle you if you did." The very softness of his voice increased the threat.

She laughed nervously. "Then why did you tell me? You could have left me in ignorance."

"You wanted to know the sort of person you are. Now you know."

"Yes," she said tremulously, going to the door.

"Wicked and wanton. But not wicked enough to hurt your mother."

"Sharon!"

She turned. "Yes?"

"Your hair," he said abruptly. "Would a hairdresser really know if it was natural?"

"Of course. Why?"

"No reason. Just curiosity." He eyed her, as if debating whether or not to say more. "Did you enjoy your ride this morning?" he went on.

"Yes. Especially when I discovered I ride very well. Simon's promised to take me out every morning."

"Don't forget he has a job to do; acting as your riding companion isn't part of it."

Sharon drew a sharp breath. "I'm sure your mother wouldn't want me to ride alone. Shall I ask her and let you know the answer?"

Grey eyes clashed with gentian blue ones and the grey were averted first.

"You win," he said icily. "Please close the door behind you."

Sharon was crossing the hall when Beryl called her. "I was looking for you, madam. There's a letter for you."

"A letter?"

Sharon took the envelope eagerly, her pulses quickening as she saw it bore a South African stamp. Aware of the maid's curious stare, she slipped it into her pocket and went up the stairs, forcing herself not to run until she had turned a bend in the corridor and no one could see her.

In the privacy of her bedroom she extracted the letter with shaking hands. There was no address, only the date, and the writing was so sprawling as to be almost illegible.

My dear Sharon,

Thank God you were saved! I can also say thank God for the crash, for when I heard it on the news and thought you'd been killed, it made me see what a skunk I was. After a bit of soul-searching I confessed the whole thing to Carol and—wait for it—she's forgiven me!

You-know-who doesn't know I've confessed and I see no reason to tell her. She'll have a fit of fury when she finds out, but thank heavens she'll no longer be able to harm me. So now the ball's in your court. I know you made a promise, but personally I think you're at liberty to call off the whole thing. I can't wait to see you, so hurry back. I won't write again till I know what your plans are. Carol sends her love and so do I, plus my undying thanks.

It was signed "Tim", but the name caused no responsive echo in her brain. She re-read the letter, hoping to make more sense of it. But it remained a mystery. The writer knew her well and for this reason had not put his address on the envelope.

Tim, Tim. She kept muttering the name, hoping to evoke some image, however slight. But all she achieved was the familiar throbbing in her head, and she put the letter away in her dressing table. Perhaps if she stopped trying to think who this mysterious man was, her subconscious might provide the answer for her.

CHAPTER FIVE

FOR the next few days Sharon puzzled over the letter. How many Tims were there in Cape Town, and could one find a man without knowing his surname? She turned over the possibility of starting enquiries, but common sense told her it was hopeless. All she could do was to hope he would write to her again when he received no reply to his letter. He might even telephone.

The thought was so exciting that each time the telephone rang during the next two weeeks, she had to force herself not to rush to answer it.

She continued to go riding each morning with Simon and though he made no further attempts to kiss her, he bombarded her with compliments.

"How would you feel about going out riding for a whole day?" he asked when they returned from one of their usual morning canters.

"Sounds lovely," she smiled, "though I'm not sure I should. Mrs. Peters wouldn't like me to be away from her the whole day."

"I'm sure she wouldn't object if you asked her."

"That's why I wouldn't ask her!"

He sighed. "You're a sharp girl behind your angelic appearance."

Sharon slid down from her horse. "Talking about appearance, when will your sister be needing her jodhpurs back? I feel guilty about wearing them so much."

"Forget it," said Simon. "She hardly ever visits me."

"What's her name?"

"Joan."

He led the horses into the stable yard and, sensing his reluctance to talk about his sister, Sharon dropped the subject, grateful she at least had one outfit that Mrs. Peters had not had to buy her.

Her mother-in-law was in excellent spirits. Being able to talk to someone about Rufus was doing her more good than any medicine, and the only disquieting factor, as far as Sharon was concerned, was that each day the woman became more dependent on her.

"I must get you a fur coat this winter," she said one afternoon as they were having tea together. "I know how badly you feel the cold."

"I won't be here in the winter," Sharon said deliberately.

"Not even for a visit? Anyway, how can you leave us when you still don't know anything about your life?"

"I know I had an apartment in Cape Town. Adam has the address on the letters I wrote to him."

"But you moved out of it when Rufus died. Don't you remember?" Mrs. Peters looked distressed. "Oh dear, of course you don't. How silly of me!"

"Don't be upset about forgetting," said Sharon. "Sometimes I forget, too. It's rather nice to think of my life beginning here with you."

"What a charming thing to say!" Mrs. Peters beamed. "I always knew you'd settle down once Adam was nicer to you."

Sharon privately considered that "nice" was hardly the right word. "Aloof" would have been a far better word to describe her brother-in-law's attitude towards her. But she held her tongue, knowing that to say what was in her heart would needlessly disturb a woman who had shown her nothing but kindness.

If only Adam was as kind! Since her conversation with him in the library, he had studiously avoided her. And she had made the same effort to avoid him: breakfasting with Mrs. Peters, not coming downstairs until she saw him striding away from the house and often lunching in her own room on the pretext that she felt tired.

Occasionally he went to London and she would catch a glimpse of him as he was driven off, sitting erect in the back of the car, reading a copy of the *Financial Times*.

It was only at dinner that she could not avoid seeing him face to face. But luckily Mrs. Peters was always there, and this forced him to a semblance of politeness, though even in front of his mother he never spoke directly to Sharon if he could help it.

Several times he dined at Helen's home, and though Sharon had told herself she was glad not to have his forbidding presence at hand, she nonetheless found her ears alert for the sound of his return. It was almost as if her dislike of him made it necessary for her to know where he was and with whom; as if, by so doing, she could stop him from mentally overwhelming her.

He was the sort of man who was always in control. He might allow passion to sway him, but it could never alter him. This thought led her swiftly to another, and she wondered how controlled he was when alone with Helen. Somehow she felt the girl's coldness was only surface-deep, and that beneath her veneer she was a deeply carnal woman, one who would respond to a man like Adam.

"What are you thinking of?" Mrs. Peters asked. "You look so serious."

"I wasn't thinking of anything," Sharon lied. "Except that I'm living a very lazy life." She yawned and stretched like a kitten. "Is Helen coming over this afternoon?"

"Yes. Was she on your mind a moment ago?" Seeing Sharon's expression, the older woman chuckled. "That didn't require much deduction on my part. When you look sour or moody, I always know you're thinking of the past or of Helen. They both tend to upset you, don't they?"

"Yes." Sharon pulled a face. "I hadn't realised I was so transparent."

"Only to me. I know you so well."

"How can you? It's only a few weeks since we met."

"Time isn't just a question of hours and weeks, my dear. It's only man who has put length to it. You can meet a person and know in an instant that they're trustworthy—or equally that they're not."

"That's a wholly feminine reply! I bet your son wouldn't agree with you."

"He doesn't like relying on his emotions. Men who feel things deeply are often afraid of doing that."

Unwilling to remain on the subject of a man who

was already occupying too much of her thoughts, Sharon leaned closer to her mother-in-law. "If you think you know me so well, tell me what kind of person I am. The truth, though, with no holds barred!"

There was a chuckle. "How easy that is! You're gentle, kind, emotional and rather impulsive. I also believe that once you love, you love for ever. Adam is like you, in that respect."

Back to Adam again. Forcibly Sharon concentrated on the assessment of herself. "I don't see myself as being all that gentle. I have quite a temper when I'm roused."

"But you're only roused when other people are cruel. You rush to defend those weaker than you. Just like Adam."

Once more he was being paraded in front of her, and this time she decided not to fight it. "I couldn't imagine Adam ever being gentle. Except with you, of course."

"And with any woman he truly loves. Once he's found her, he'll be putty in her hands. At one stage I thought he'd found her in Helen, but now I'm not so sure." The soft voice sank lower. "He needs someone with more tenderness, someone more like—"

Abruptly Sharon pushed back her chair and stood up.

"How about a stroll?" she suggested. "It's a lovely afternoon."

Together they walked across the lawn to the lake. Willows arched their branches over the water, lowering their green fingers to touch their own shimmering reflections. A golden Labrador bounded up to them and Sharon bent to pat him, fondling the floppy ears. It was

Adam's dog and the animal rarely left his side when he was at home.

"Good Sandy," she said. "Fetch your ball."

The dog disappeared among the bushes and emerged holding a bright red ball in his mouth. He dropped it at her feet and barked, his tail waving like a flag.

"If you'd like to take him for a run," Mrs. Peters suggested, "I'll be quite happy to sit on the terrace. I'm afraid to walk along with him; he's inclined to jump up at me."

"I won't be long," Sharon promised. "I'll just go down to the spinney and back."

She raced over the grass, the dog bounding at her side. Once among the trees they both slowed their pace; Sandy snuffling interestedly around the tree roots and Sharon enjoying the patterns of light made by the green canopy of leaves above her head.

After a while she settled on an overturned trunk and idly threw Sandy's ball for him until finally, pink tongue lolling, he sank down by her side. Almost at once the hair on his neck bristled and he growled as a woman in a mauve dress came through the trees. With dismay, Sharon recognised Helen.

"Hello there," Helen said pleasantly. "Exercising the dog?"

"Yes."

"Then we can walk back to the house together. This is a short cut. I use it when I don't have the car."

"Is your home far from here?" Sharon asked.

"Less than a mile. You must come to dinner before you leave."

"I'm not thinking of leaving yet," Sharon lied.

"Adam said you were. But then he's so anxious for you to go he's probably making himself believe you will. Speaking personally, I think you'll hang on here as long as you can."

"You like speaking personally, don't you?" Sharon said coldly.

Helen shrugged and said, "Please don't think I blame you. If I were in your shoes, I'd probably do the same. After all, you have a wonderful home here with all the luxuries a woman like you thinks necessary."

"Don't *you*?"

"Naturally. But I'd give something in return."

Sharon quickened her pace. "It's no concern of yours when I go. I suggest you mind your own business."

"It is my business! Your being here reminds Adam that I used to be engaged to Rufus, which is something he'd rather forget. If it weren't for you, we'd have announced our engagement by now."

"What a pity," Sharon snapped, angered by the thought that it was only her presence here that prevented him from asking this hard-faced young woman to marry him.

"But it will happen sooner or later," Helen continued, "so don't bother trying to get him for yourself."

"He's the last man I want!"

"You don't give that impression. I've noticed the big-eyed way you look at him."

"If I never saw him again I'd be delighted," Sharon retorted.

"Then why don't you pack your bags and go? You don't need to worm your way any deeper into Mrs. Peters's affections. You know very well she'll remember you in her will."

"I couldn't care less about her will!"

"Then get out. Don't you know you're not wanted here?" Whirling on her heel, Helen strode towards the house.

Watching the tall figure with its straight shoulders and narrow hips, the sensibly clad feet marching so resolutely over the grass, Sharon could understand why a weak man like Rufus had been attracted to Helen. But she failed to see what Adam admired in her. She was not the right wife for him. Married to her, he would become more autocratic and domineering in order to maintain his independence. He needed a woman who would tease him and make him laugh, give him affection as well as passion, someone who was gentle and kind and impulsive.

Aghast, she stopped. What had made her use those three adjectives? The reason was painfully clear and she could no longer avoid admitting it. She loved Adam. She loved him and could not bear to think of him marrying anyone except herself.

A deep sigh escaped her. Fat chance she had, when he made no secret of the fact that he despised her, that he blamed her for encouraging Rufus to ruin his life.

Intent on reaching the privacy of her room, she hurried across the terrace. But as she reached the French windows, Beryl rushed forward.

"Thank goodness you're back," she exclaimed. "The mistress is ill!"

Sharon's throat contracted. "Where is she?"

"Cook and I carried her to her home and Miss Helen phoned for Mr. Adam. He was at Mr. Lennox's house."

"Have you called the doctor?"

"Mr. Adam said he'd bring him along."

Steps in the hall confirmed Beryl's answer and, through the half-open door, Sharon saw Adam and an elderly man moving towards the stairs.

"It was probably a heart attack," Helen said matter-of-factly. "She's had them before."

Beryl gasped and Sharon gave the maid's arm a reassuring squeeeze. The girl was from the village and had known Mrs. Peters all her life. It was understandable for her to be upset.

After what seemed an endless wait but could not have been more than a quarter of an hour, Adam and the doctor entered the drawing room, with Helen close behind them.

"A mild heart attack," the doctor said to the room at large. "She must stay in bed for a couple of weeks and have no excitement." He looked at Adam. "I can rely on you for that?"

"Naturally."

"May I go and see her?" Helen asked.

Adam shook his head. "She's asking for Sharon."

Ignoring Helen's look of dislike, Sharon hurried into the hall. As she reached the stairs Adam came out of the drawing room and called her. Then he closed the door behind him and walked forward.

"Mother said just now that you'd been talking of leaving. I know I asked you to go, but—well, for the moment it would be better if you remained."

"If you wish. I don't want to do anything that would upset her."

Sharon looked at him and then lowered her eyes. Intensely conscious of his nearness, she saw his hands, narrow and strong, clenching and unclenching at his sides. How he hated asking her to stay!

"If I remain here until your mother has recovered," she said carefully, "I will expect you to behave politely to me."

"I'll do my best," he said coldly.

"Is there nothing I can do to change your opinion of me?" she cried. "What if I said I didn't want any money from you or your mother?"

"I wouldn't believe it." His glance took in her plain but expensive silk dress, worn with a gold necklet his mother had given her as a surprise the previous day.

"What if I gave you my word?" she persisted.

"I'd assume you'd have some other plan in mind!" His eyes were slivers of grey ice. "If only I knew what —" With a weary gesture he motioned her to go upstairs. "Mother's waiting for you."

"What were you going to say?" Sharon asked. "I've a right to know."

"All right!" With an effort he controlled himself. "Perhaps you have, at that. But not until my mother's recovered. In the meantime, though, you can tell me something."

"Whatever you like," she said bitterly. "You know as much about me as I know about myself."

"Then tell me what you hope to gain by seeing so much of Simon."

Colour rushed into her cheeks. "He's the only person here, apart from your mother, who's shown me any kindness."

"You'd do well to keep away from him."

"Why?"

"Let's say it's for your own good."

"Don't tell me you care about that?" she mocked, and saw a flame of anger flash in his pupils before he spun on his heels and returned to the drawing room.

Mrs. Peters was propped up by pillows when Sharon saw her, but otherwise looked no different from when they had last been together.

"A lot of fuss over nothing," she complained as Sharon perched on the bed. "It was only a mild attack."

"Enough to warrant your taking better care of yourself."

"I loathe staying in bed," sighed Mrs. Peters.

"I'll be here to keep you company," Sharon consoled her.

"You mean you won't be leaving?"

"Not until you're completely well." Sharon smiled as she saw Mrs. Peters's expression. "But I'll know if you start pretending, so don't put on an act."

"What a thing to suggest!"

Happily the old lady closed her eyes, opening them from time to time to see if Sharon was still there.

The afternoon passed slowly and it was only when

Beryl came in with a nurse that Sharon felt free to leave the room.

"I'll be in to see you before you go to sleep for the night," she promised her mother-in-law. "But if you want to see me before, let the nurse know."

Downstairs, she was relieved to find the drawing room empty except for Sandy, who was stretched full-length on the rug in front of the fireplace. Absentmindedly she stooped to pat him, then wandered restlessly from one piece of furniture to another, looking at each with all her attention but seeing only Adam's face. It was ironic that she should have fallen in love with a man she hardly knew, a man who had shown her nothing but contempt. Even his ideas and beliefs were a closed book to her, as she was a closed book to herself.

But no, that wasn't true about herself or him. Though much of him remained an enigma, she knew him to be honest, kind to those he loved and an excellent employer. As for her own character, she might not know how she had felt or what she had done in the past, but she was quite aware of her reactions in the here and now. As for her emotions, there was no doubt that a man like Adam, who even had the dark looks she so admired, had always been her ideal.

Always? Then how could she have fallen in love with a fair-haired, morally weak man like Rufus?

Idly her hand roamed over the keyboard of the piano she had come to rest against, and without conscious thought she sat down on the piano stool and began to play—first a Chopin prelude, then a sparkling piece of Vivaldi. Only as the last notes died away was she aware of Adam watching her, his face set in such hard lines that it resembled a mask. But the eyes were alive, glittering like the eyes of a bird of prey.

"So you play the piano," he said harshly. "May I ask what other accomplishments you have?"

"I only discovered I had this one a moment ago."

"You're no amateur."

"No," she agreed. "I'm rather pleased with the way I play."

"Have you no shame at all?" He slammed the lid shut with such force that he almost caught her fingers. "If it weren't for my mother, I'd throw you out of the house tonight!"

Astonished, she looked at him. "Because I play the piano?"

"Because you're playing me for a fool!" He drew back a step, as if being close to her might goad him into physical violence. "At the moment, you're in a stronger position than I am. But don't try me too far. If you do, even my mother won't stop me from exposing you!"

Before she could ask him what he meant, he strode out, banging the door so violently that the chandelier tinkled.

"Expose me?" Sharon whispered, wondering if she would make more sense out of his comment if she said it aloud. Expose that she was here to get money? That she had come to wheedle herself into her mother-in-law's grace?

Somehow she didn't think so. Adam had meant more than this. Much more. But what it was and when she would find out were two things she didn't know.

CHAPTER SIX

SHARON'S dreams that night were tortuous; not quite nightmares yet with an undercurrent of horror that made her wake up several times, trembling. But once consciousness returned she could not bring them to mind. All she could recall was the fear; the people and situations behind it remained a blur.

At six o'clock she switched on her lamp, having made up her mind it was better to be awake than to sleep in torment. She tried to keep her mind blank, but an image of Adam, his face suffused with rage, shimmered in front of her. Why had playing the piano roused him to such anger that he had threatened to throw her out of the house? But no matter how deeply she searched for an answer, it eluded her.

At eight-thirty she tapped at the door of her mother-in-law's room, relieved when the nurse opened it with a smile and beckoned her in.

"We've had a very good night," she announced briskly, "and we're feeling much better, aren't we, dear?"

"Yes, we are," Mrs. Peters assented, smiling wryly at Sharon as the nurse turned away.

"I wasn't sure if it was too early for me to come in," Sharon murmured, bending to kiss the lined cheek.

"From the look of you, you could have come in hours ago! Didn't you sleep?"

"Not too well."

"Were you reliving the plane crash?"

"I don't remember anything about it—which is just as well."

"I'm not so sure," said Mrs Peters. "I think it's necessary to remember painful things in order to forget them. Running from something we're afraid to face can turn it into more of a horror."

Sharon wondered if there was a hidden meaning behind this remark. Was Mrs. Peters hinting that she knew some of the things Rufus had done? But it was not her business to find out. That was up to Adam.

Sipping her coffee, Sharon studied her mother-in-law. If it were not for the telltale bluish line around her lips, one would never know she had a heart condition.

"Has Adam been up to see you yet?" she asked.

"He looked in for a moment just before you came. He's going to London on business and won't be back until this evening."

Involuntarily Sharon heaved a sigh of relief, then glanced quickly towards the bed to see if it had been noticed. But Mrs. Peters was folding her napkin and replacing it in its ring.

"Are you going riding today?" she asked.

"No. Simon said he'd be busy."

"Why don't you go for a walk?" The old woman's gaze wandered to the window. "It's such a lovely day."

"Sounds like a good idea. I'll come in and see you when I get back."

Sharon was halfway down the stairs before she

noticed, through the open front door, the Bentley parked at the foot of the steps. So Adam had not left yet! She hesitated, reluctant to meet him again but more reluctant to admit her fear of him by running away. He must never know how he affected her, never guess that her bones seemed to melt at the sight of him.

She became aware of raised voices in the library and recognised Adam's deep one and the slightly higher-pitched tone of Simon.

"I don't care what you think!" the bailiff was saying. "I'll tell her in my own good time."

"If you had any guts you'd tell her now!" Adam was angrier than Sharon had ever heard him.

"I want to give her a chance to know me better," Simon retorted. "When I think she cares for me, I'll tell her the truth. I love her and I'm not going to run the risk of losing her."

"You hardly know her."

"I've been riding with her nearly every morning since she's been here."

"You'd have done better to fall for the mare!"

Simon's chuckle showed he had not taken the comment seriously, though when next he spoke there was no humour in his voice.

"I can't stop you from telling her, Adam, and if you—"

"I'm no informer!" Adam barked.

"I didn't think you were." There was no mistaking Simon's relief. "But I'll understand if you want my resignation."

"Don't be a fool! You're the best bailiff I've had and no woman is going to make me lose you. The only time I'll ask you to move on is if Sharon returns your love and agrees to marry you."

There was a shout of laughter. "You've the darnedest way of thinking! I'll remember that when I ask you to be best man!"

There were sounds of footsteps and Sharon shrank against the banister as the two men crossed the hall and went outside.

"Can I give you a lift back to the cottage?" she heard Adam ask.

"You can drop me off in the village. I want to buy some stamps."

The car door slammed and the Bentley purred down the drive. Only then did Sharon go down the stairs and into the garden.

What had Adam urged Simon to tell her? Undoubtedly it was something to do with his past, something so detrimental he was afraid she would despise him if she found out. As if she had the right to despise anyone when she herself—according to Adam—was so despicable!

As she wended her way to the village she decided she was glad to have overheard the conversation. But she mustn't let Simon know. Instead she would start to make excuses not to see him and, on the few occasions when she did, would make it clear she regarded him only as a friend.

How complicated everything was! If Mrs. Peters was well, Sharon could have left Green Spinney that very day and have started looking for a job. Then, as soon as she saved up the fare, she could return to South Africa and try to find out something of her past and the life she had lived with Rufus.

When she reached the village she looked around for Simon. He was not in the post office-cum-general store and she glanced across at the painted sign of a ferocious black bull that hung over the door of the Tudor-style inn. This was the place Helen had accused him of visiting too often.

No sooner had she thought this than she saw him coming out of it with a young woman. She was too far away to hear what they were saying, but it was obvious they were arguing. The woman was gesticulating wildly and Simon caught hold of her and pulled her along the road to where a small blue car was parked. He bundled her in, then climbed in himself and drove out of sight.

Was that Simon's sister? She had the same blonde hair, though it appeared that nature had been given some assistance, and her clothes were more suited to town than country. One might almost have called them flashy: the black suit a shade too tight, the gold jewellery at throat and wrist a shade too heavy.

Sharon continued her walk, wondering why Simon had not mentioned that his sister was here. Could that be the reason he and Adam had quarrelled?

But the rest of the day passed without Simon putting in an appearance, and Sharon spent the time with her mother-in-law.

As twilight fell a car could be heard coming up the drive. Mrs. Peters smiled happily.

"Adam's back. I hope he brought me the—" She stopped abruptly, but her hands played restlessly with the edge of the blanket.

"I'll go and change," said Sharon. "I'll come back later."

"Don't go yet. I want you to wait till Adam comes up."

This was exactly what Sharon had wanted to avoid and she bit back a sigh. Soon they heard firm steps approaching along the corridor and the door opened. As always when she saw Adam after an absence, Sharon was struck by the strength he exuded and wished with all her heart it was not directed against her.

"How are you, Mother?" He drew her hand to his lips.

"Much better, darling. Did you bring it back with you?"

"Yes." He took a flat leather box from his pocket and placed it on the bed.

"Come here, Sharon," Mrs. Peters urged. "I want to show you something."

Sharon did as she was told and found herself staring at a triple row of exquisitely matched pink pearls. "They're beautiful!" she breathed.

"My husband gave them to me when Adam was born and I promised myself that one day I would give them to his bride."

Sharon felt her colour recede. So Helen had finally achieved her ambition. With an effort she looked at Adam.

"Congratulations! When's the happy day?"

"I don't know what you're talking about."

"Adam!" his mother reproached. "What a rude way to answer!" She looked at Sharon. "It's my fault really. I expressed myself badly. Although I'd promised to give these pearls to Adam's wife, as soon as *you* came into my life, I knew I couldn't give them to anyone else. So this morning I asked Adam's permission to give them to you."

"You didn't need my permission," he said briskly. "The pearls are yours to do with as you please."

"I know that. But if you'd been upset by it—"

"No!" Sharon cut in wildly. "I can't accept them. Absolutely not!"

"Of course you can," Mrs. Peters held them out. "Please, my dear, put them on."

Sharon remained motionless. Without being able to explain why, she felt it impossible to accept this gift that represented so much more than money.

"I can't!" she repeated.

Silently Adam took the pearls from his mother's hand and advanced on Sharon. "Turn around and let me fasten them for you."

There was something about the set of his mouth that made her obey. She turned her back to him and felt the pearls cool around her throat. His fingers fumbled at the nape of her neck. Their touch was warm on her skin and she trembled and jerked away from him.

"Let me see them on you," Mrs. Peters called, and blindly Sharon stepped close to the bed. "Your skin has the same translucence as the pearls. They're exactly right for you. Don't you think so, Adam?"

"Yes," he said expressionlessly. "Now if you'll excuse me, Mother, I want to wash and change."

"Is Helen coming over?" she asked.

"No. She went to Paris this morning. An aunt of hers has been taken ill there."

"In that case why don't you take Sharon out dancing? She hasn't been anywhere since she came here."

"I'm perfectly happy to stay with you," Sharon protested.

"Well, you shouldn't be. You're a young woman and it's time you started enjoying yourself again. It isn't right for you to—to mourn Rufus for ever. And he wouldn't want it, either." The voice quavered. "He was always so full of life, so charming and—"

"You're quite right Mother," Adam interrupted. "I'll take Sharon out and she'll be able to tell you how much she enjoyed herself!" He opened the door and waited for Sharon to go with him.

Outside the bedroom she looked at him with hostility.

"You can cut the pretence. I'll dine in my room and make up some story to tell your mother in the morning."

"And where will you say I took you? You don't know the district; you wouldn't fool her for a second."

"Can't you describe a place to me?"

"No." He pulled her roughly away from the door. "I'm not taking you out because I want to, but because I don't want to upset my mother."

"Nor do I," Sharon flared. "The sooner she's better the sooner I'll be able to leave here."

"Then we understand one another! Now get changed and meet me downstairs in an hour."

Despite the anger he aroused in her, she dressed with great care, discarding two outfits before settling on a third. She was fifteen minutes late when she gave herself a final appraisal, happy that the black, paper-silk taffeta dress made her look lovelier than he had ever seen her. The bodice was severely plain, with a deep décolletage and narrow straps marking her creamy shoulders, while from the tiny, nipped-in waist, the skirt billowed into innumerable frills, each one lifting as she walked.

"It's a dream of a dress," Monsieur Duval had said when she had chosen it. "Meant for dancing and loving!"

Remembering this, she was tempted to change into something else, only prevented from doing so by her lateness. Picking up her bag and an emerald satin coat, she sped down the stairs.

Adam was waiting in the hall and, hearing the rustle of her dress, turned to watch her. For a moment he was unable to guard his expression and she thrilled to see the naked desire on his face. Despise her though he did, he wanted her!

But in an instant he was in control of himself, and his voice cold as he said, "You're late."

She shrugged and followed him to the Bentley. She slid into the front seat and he slammed the door after her so heavily that her skirts lifted.

What an evening this was going to be, she thought, watching him from beneath her lashes as he took the wheel. He wore a midnight blue dinner jacket, so dark as to be almost black. Its colour was a subtle echo of his blue-black hair, which, though severely flattened, had still not lost its slight wave. A curving strand fell upon his forehead and her fingers ached to touch it.

In silence they moved down the drive. The car purred along quietly and she was lulled into a false sense of contentment, willing herself to believe she was sitting beside a man who returned her affections and would not spurn her.

Some ten minutes after leaving Green Spinney Adam turned into the entrance of a large hotel. A long line of cars was parked outside, but he stopped at the entrance, gave the keys to a waiting attendant and escorted her into a carpeted foyer.

"Would you like to leave your coat?" he asked.

"I'll keep it," she replied. "It looks rather striking, don't you think?"

"You're striking enough," he said curtly, and steered her none too gently into the bar that lay off to one side of the lobby. The room was full of laughing groups of people, and there was a great deal of noise. It was not the sort of place Sharon had associated with Adam and she was surprised he had brought her here.

"Don't you like it?" he asked.

"It's rather – er – garish."

"Rufus said you liked bright lights and noise."

She bit her lip, determined to keep her temper. "I can't believe I'd like them as bright or as noisy as this."

Busy trying to catch the waiter's attention, Adam ignored her remark. "What will you drink?" he asked.

"Champagne," she said defiantly. "I'm sure that fits your picture of me!"

He raised his eyebrows. "Have milk if you prefer."

"I'll stick to champagne. We might as well celebrate our first evening out. It's bound to be our last."

Again he did not respond but gave his order to the waiter and leaned back in his chair. Of all the men in the bar he was the most handsome, and many feminine eyes were cast in his direction. He appeared oblivious to them, lost in some world of his own.

Sharon was debating how much longer she could remain here in silence without kicking him on the ankle when he abruptly spoke.

"My mother's extremely fond of you."

"I know. It means a great deal to me."

"I'm sure it does."

"Not for the reasons you think," she said flatly. "But when you're alone in a strange country, it's good to know someone cares for you."

"I should imagine a great many people have cared for you," he replied. "It wouldn't be difficult."

"Wouldn't it? You seem to find it difficult."

"I see you in a different way."

"It could be the wrong way," she pointed out.

"I don't think so. I see the woman behind the lovely face, the true character lying behind those heavenly blue eyes." His jaw set pugnaciously. "My God! It's hard to believe you're a—"

Just then an icebucket and champagne was set before them, and he broke off and signalled the waiter to fill their glasses. Only as he lifted his own did he resume talking.

"What shall our toast be? To the future? To your memory returning? Or perhaps to your memory not returning?"

"Not that! You surely don't think I like living in a vacuum?"

"I don't know what you like," he shrugged.

"I'm only gradually finding that out myself. But why not accept me as I am? Take me at face value."

"At face value you're extremely beautiful."

Her heart leaped. "Am I really?"

"You know damn well you are," he said harshly. "A beautiful and alluring woman." There was a pause. "How many men have you had?"

The cold-bloodedness of the question shook her. Her fingers trembled around her glass and she was afraid she might spill some of the liquid and so give herself away. But luckily she didn't, and hoped he hadn't noticed the tremor.

"I can't remember." How calm her voice sounded! With an effort she stared into his eyes, noticing the short but amazingly thick lashes surrounding them. "What about you? Or have you lost count of your affairs?"

"I'm thirty-three," he stated. "Old enough to have had enough. I now find casual affairs boring."

"So what's next? Marriage?"

"One day it will have to be. I want a son."

So matter-of-fact was the statement that Sharon was

surprised at the intensity with which it hit her. Adam and his son. If only it could be her son, too.

"I don't think there's any point continuing this conversation, Sharon. When you've finished your drink we'll go in and eat."

The dining room, like the bar, was elaborately decorated. Snow-white cloths were covered with an abundance of silver and cut glass; candles and flowers added to the lavishness. The food followed the same standard and Sharon made a great effort to eat what was set before her, reluctant to let Adam guess how much his aloofness hurt her.

Throughout the dinner he maintained a minimum of conversation and though there were long pauses while they waited for their various courses to arrive, he did not ask her to dance. When their coffee was served, an imp of mischief—or could it have been temper?—prompted her to suggest it herself.

"Your mother's sure to ask me if we did," she said without any expression in her voice, "and she'll be surprised if I say no. Or perhaps you don't dance at all?"

"Yes, I do," he said through clenched teeth, and pushed back his chair.

As they reached the floor the tempo of the music slowed to a languorous beat. Adam muttered under his breath and, with a thrill of pleasure, Sharon knew he was afraid of the emotion this type of rhythm might awaken in him. She moved into his arms and felt him stiffen, as if her closeness disturbed him. But of course it did. He found her an alluring woman—he had said so. And he was a virile, sensual man, his restraint but a sign of the strong passions he was holding in check. Had he been willing to let his natural inclinations come to the fore, he would now be doing everything to encourage a love affair between them.

If she could only get beneath his guard, the way she had a few weeks ago when he kissed her, she might be able to make him revise his opinion of her, or at least make him give her a chance to show him she was not the heartless, mercenary creature Rufus had depicted.

Involuntarily her fingers touched the back of his neck. She felt him tremble, hold back for an instant and then pull her closer. His cheek brushed her hair and she savoured the warmth of his breath on her temple, the steel-like hardness of his thighs pressing upon her own, the thudding of his heart, its beat so heavy it was like insistent fingertips drumming upon her breast.

"Let's get out of here." He drew away sharply. "I've had enough."

She nodded. Tears were an eyeblink away and she knew if she released them, he would guess her secret. Head high, she followed him to the car.

Though it was a beautiful starry night, she sat shivering in the corner. Adam switched on the heater and they drove down the tree-lined avenue to the highway. In silence they sped along the country lanes, twisting tortuously in and out of narrow turnings. Adam drove with a controlled violence that both excited and frightened her, his hands gripping the wheel as if gripping her throat. Intuitively she knew that he hated her for making him aware of his weakness, that he would give anything to get her out of his system.

They rounded another bend and Green Spinney lay ahead, its outline large in the moonlight. They skirted the front of the house and pulled to a stop in the large garage at the back.

"Damn you!" Adam grated, and reached out for her.

Sharon made no attempt to evade him. Instead she melted against his body, pliant as velvet beneath his searching hands. Uncaring of the consequences, she opened herself to him—arms widening to hold him, lips parting to absorb the moisture of his kisses.

In a frenzy of passion they clasped one another. He rained kisses on her face, her neck, her shoulders, gentle yet urgent kisses that made her cry out with longing. He unbuttoned his shirt and her hands caressed his chest, feeling its satiny texture and the roughness of the dark hair that covered part of it. Then she responded with kisses of her own, revelling in the strength of his body but knowing that, at this moment, her own strength was the greater.

"I want you so much." His voice was a torment of desire, the words partly stifled as he strained her closer. "Don't say no, Sharon. Come to me, darling."

She'd thought herself powerless to resist him, but suddenly, without warning, she knew it was impossible to surrender. It had to be with love; it had to be with gentleness, understanding, reciprocation. Passion, no matter how strong, and technical prowess, no matter how proficient, were nothing compared with the hesitations and fumblings of tender, genuine love.

"I—I can't," she gasped. "Don't make me."

As if in slow motion Adam drew back. Although she could not see his face clearly, she sensed the ebbing of his passion that, like a triumphant conqueror, had urged him on to a final victory. Now the victory was denied and she waited fearfully for the backlash of his anger. But nothing came; only his voice as gentle as a drifting snowflake, and just as icy.

"I'm grateful to you, Sharon. You've saved me from despising myself." He opened the car door and averted his face from her as if not wishing to see her disarray.

"I don't feel I owe you an apology," he continued. "You asked for what you got. Although praise be, in the final analysis, you had the sense not to want it!"

CHAPTER SEVEN

HAD it not been for her promise to Mrs. Peters, Sharon would not have spent another night under the same roof as Adam. How could he believe her to be so heartless when she had sufficient conscience not to leave his mother?

He would say it was because she had her eye on the main chance and wanted Mrs. Peters to go on liking her, but Sharon knew this was untrue. She had never cared about possessions or money for herself; it was only when it came to—

Her thoughts stopped, as though cut off by a blank wall she could not penetrate. Only when it came to what? If she didn't want money for herself, for whom had she been trying to get it? Was it to help someone else that she had asked for and accepted money from Adam, after Rufus had been killed? And what of her behaviour during Rufus's lifetime? Was it possible he had blackened her character deliberately? Had he wanted Adam to think she was mercenary when it had been himself all along? But that couldn't be true. For it didn't explain the letter she had written to Adam, threatening to come to England on a visit and tell his mother all about Rufus unless he sent her some money.

In an effort to forget her inner turmoil, she put on her riding clothes and went downstairs. She knew her mother-in-law would be anxious to hear about the previous night, but could not face the lies she would have to utter. She would leave it till later, when a gallop had blown away some of her tension.

But seeing Simon was also going to be a strain, for she still had to tell him she regarded him only as a friend. He was waiting for her outside the stables, the horses saddled and ready.

"No one would think you'd had a late night," he greeted her.

"How do you know I did?"

He helped her into the saddle. "I saw Adam this morning. He had a vile headache and said he'd drunk too much."

"He hardly drank anything," Sharon protested.

"Well, whatever it was, it went to his head!"

Simon mounted his own horse and they trotted slowly down the drive. "It's going to be a marvellous day. What do you say we go to Vernon Hill? You haven't seen the view from there yet, and I've been promising myself to show it to you."

Without waiting for her answer he dug his heels into his horse's sides and cantered ahead of her. They rode across country for several miles, and the feel of the breeze in her hair raised Sharon's spirits somewhat. It was impossible to be downcast when on horseback, and she looked affectionately at the glossy neck below her.

When at last they reached the top of Vernon Hill they drew rein. She slid to the ground, laughing breathlessly. "That was wonderful, Simon! I needed the workout as much as Gilda!"

He took the reins from her and tied them to a nearby

bush. "She hates being cooped up, and I was too busy to exercise her yesterday."

"I saw you in the village with your sister," Sharon said casually.

"My sister?" Simon concentrated on tying up his own horse. "Where was that?"

"You were coming out of the Bull and drove off before I could speak to you. I wanted to ask if she needed her clothes back."

"No, she doesn't." He turned slowly. "Jane hardly rides these days."

"I thought her name was Joan?"

"You must be muddling her up with someone else." He caught Sharon's arm and swivelled her around to look at the view. "Wasn't it worth the journey?"

She nodded and followed the line of his finger to the country stretched out below. The sun shone on vivid green and gold fields, and in the far distance the motorway, tiny black cars speeding along it, was a snaking silver-grey ribbon.

"It makes one feel like a dictator," she said. "As if you could control everything."

"What an awful thought!" he laughed. "I'd hate to be in control."

"I wouldn't have thought so. You've always struck me as being strong, with a very good sense of what's right."

"You make me sound like a bit of a prig," he commented.

"Oh no," she disagreed. "You'd be the last person to condemn anyone."

"I should hope so. Live and let live is my motto."

"It's mine, too." Remembering his conversation with Adam, she was anxious to tell him he need have no fear in confiding in her. "I don't believe one has the right to judge anyone else. A person is governed by so many inner motivations that, unless you know what they are, you can't even begin to understand."

"What's all this talk about judging and understanding?" Simon asked. "You're far too serious for such a lovely morning. Sit down and enjoy this view."

She did so, liking the sensation of the soft turf beneath her. She yawned.

"My late night's catching up on me. The ride has tired me."

"Have a catnap." He sat beside her. "I'll keep guard and ward off the wild animals—particularly wolves!"

Sharon laughed and closed her eyes. The breeze had dropped and everything was still; the only sound that reached her was the noise of the horses cropping the grass a few yards away. How peaceful it was! How happy she could be if only— She heaved a sigh and drifted off to sleep.

She awoke with a start to see Simon bending over her; she sat up hurriedly.

"Have I been asleep long?" she asked.

"Half an hour."

"How boring for you!"

"To watch you? I've loved it."

She made a movement to stand, but he detained her.

"Wait, Sharon. I want to talk to you."

"It's late," she said. "We must go home."

"Not yet."

He rolled over and forced her back on the ground. His body pressed hers and his lips found her mouth. For an instant she lay passive, hoping her lack of response would be sufficient warning. But he went on kissing her and her annoyance rose. This was the second time within twenty-four hours she had been kissed by force, but whereas the first occasion had been bittersweet, this time she couldn't wait to be free. She pushed against Simon, but he did not release her. His muscles were like steel, and her annoyance turned to anger.

"Let me go!"

She almost shouted the order that was accompanied by another furious heave against his chest. He released her abruptly and stood up, his face pale, his breathing heavy.

"I'm sorry, Sharon. I—I couldn't help myself. You're so lovely and I want you so much. From the minute I saw you I fell in love with you. I want to marry you."

"I don't love you." The words were curt, but she was too angry to be kind. "I've never given you any cause to think I do."

"Is there someone else?"

"No."

"Are you sure?"

"What business is it of yours anyway?" she demanded. "You're as bad as Adam!"

"I thought you'd mention Adam sooner or later. You can't talk five minutes without bringing his name into the conversation. He's the one you love, isn't he?"

"Don't make wild guesses. I hardly know him. Now if you'll excuse me, I'm going home!" She ran to her horse and, before he could help her, sprang into the saddle. She was almost within sight of Green Spinney when he caught up with her, and together they rode the last few hundred yards to the stables, where she dismounted and handed him her bridle.

"Goodbye, Simon," she said, turning to go.

"Will I see you at the same time tomorrow?" he asked.

"No. I won't be riding with you any more."

"Because I kissed you?" His face contorted. "I give you my word it won't happen again. Anyway, it's no insult to ask a woman to marry you. It's usually considered a compliment."

"It was a compliment, Simon, but it's better for both of us if I don't ride with you again."

"You may change your mind when you've simmered down," he replied, as he led the horses away.

Sharon spent the rest of the day with her mother-in-law. Mrs. Peters wanted to hear everything about the previous evening, and Sharon did her best to make it seeem as if she and Adam had had a wonderful time.

"You must get him to take you out more often," the older woman said. "It's good for both of you.

Sharon nodded dutifully, without any intention of obeying. She could barely face the prospect of seeing him again, let alone going out with him.

In order to avoid meeting Adam that evening, she pleaded a headache and had dinner sent to her room. But as the hours passed the lie became a reality, so she undressed and went to bed, her head throbbing more violently than ever as she lay between the sheets.

Some time after nine she heard Adam's car drive away and assumed he had gone to see Helen. The thought only made her headache worse, and grimly she acknowledged the power of jealousy and what it could do. At last the pain drove her to the bathroom for aspirin. She swallowed a couple and, returning to her room, opened the window and leaned her elbows on the sill to breathe deeply of the cool night air. She had lain in bed longer than she had supposed, for the moon was high in the sky and the intense stillness told her everybody had long since gone to sleep. But she had not heard Adam return and her eyes were drawn to the belt of trees on her left, beyond which was the road leading to Helen's house.

A sudden noise from the far side of the lawn made her lift her head sharply. She remained motionless, listening. Then she heard it again, this time louder. It sounded like the whinnying of horses, and she strained her eyes into the darkness. The noise came again and her heart pounded as she saw a thin wisp of smoke rising above the trees.

The stables were on fire!

Without pausing to think, she pulled on her dressing gown and raced down the stairs out of the house. It was only as she neared the stables and saw the smoke pouring from the building that she regretted her impulsiveness. She should have had the sense to awaken the servants and tell them to call for help. But to run back to the house now would delay things even further.

She was still hesitating when a tongue of flame shot out of the stable door. Her indecisiveness vanished and she rushed forward, her own fear forgotten as she heard the sounds of even greater fear from the horses trapped in their stalls. They were neighing in terror and beating their hooves against the walls. Holding an arm over her face in a vain effort to stave off the thick smoke billowing everywhere, she entered the stable and fumbled with the bolt on the first stall. It was stiff and she tried not to panic at her inability to move it. Gripping it again, she gave it a sharp tug. As her skin rasped painfully on the wood the bolt slid back and she flung the door open and jumped aside as a panic-stricken horse rushed out, hooves flying, head tossing as it cantered to safety.

There were three more box stalls to open and Sharon drew a tearful breath as she saw Gilda was in the next one, the white star on her forehead blazing in the light of the flames. She tried to shout reassurance to the animal, but her voice, thick with the acrid smoke belching around her, came out as a croak. Abandoning efforts to calm the creature, she concentrated on setting her free.

By the time the last horse had galloped to safety, its eyes rolling with fright, Sharon was hardly able to see. The smoke was no longer grey but black, with a sharp smell that caught at her throat and made breathing difficult. Her eyes were streaming and half-closed as she stumbled to the door and safety.

She was on the threshold when a whinney drew her back. Or did the cry come from one of the horses already outside? Did Adam have four animals or five? Wildly she looked in the direction of the house, hoping someone had seen the fire and was coming to her aid—except that no one knew she was here. But surely they would come running to set the horses free? Not the maids, perhaps, but Jenkins, the elderly man who cleaned the silver and did the odd jobs.

A horse whinnied again, a cry of terror that left her no choice but to return and try to save it. Pulling a handkerchief from her pocket, she tied it around her mouth and plunged into what had now become a flame-belching inferno. Tongues of fire licked the walls and shot out scarlet fingers to catch her. One singed the hem of her dressing gown, and in alarm she drew it up with one hand, holding her other hand to her face. Tears blurred her vision and she half closed her eyes and peered ahead, no longer sure of her bearings. Would the horse be in a stall to the left or to the right of her? Or was it at the far end—and where *was* the end of the stables? Was she still facing the door or had she turned after entering?

She was still hesitating when a saw-edged flame leaped out and singed her hand. With a cry of pain she jumped back. Her foot caught on something behind her and she stumbled. She half turned to save herself, but as her hands reached out for a hold, another flame shot towards her. With a scream she put her hands to protect her face. The movement of her arms increased the momentum of her lurch and sent her crashing to the floor. Her head struck a hard object and sharp pain seared through her. She gasped, cried out and then felt herself sinking into a darkness from which there was no escape.

CHAPTER EIGHT

"SHARON! Sharon darling, can you hear me? Darling, speak to me. Say something!" It was a man's voice and the pain in it echoed the pain exploding in her head.

"Sharon—darling!" Again the voice spoke her name and this time she knew it was Adam. But why was he so distraught, and why had he called her darling?

Her eyes flew open and stared into grey ones so close to hers that she saw the darker flecks in them. Instantly the eyes receded and the rest of the face came into focus: Adam's face, pale with fear.

"Lie still," he said as she gasped and tried to sit up.

"The horses!" she cried. "Were they all saved? I thought I heard one in—".

"They're all out," he said swiftly. "Now lie still."

Firm hands applied gentle pressure upon her, forcing her back; she realised she was lying on her own bed.

"You were magnificent," Adam went on. "Though why you didn't raise the alarm instead of rushing into the stables on your own—"

"I didn't think of it till I was already there. And then I was afraid to waste time by going back to the house. I had to save the horses." Once more she tried to sit up. "I heard a fifth one, but I couldn't find it. What—?"

"It wasn't there. I rode it over to Helen's a couple of days ago and he went lame on the way, so I left him there."

"You mean I went back into the stables for nothing?" She started to laugh weakly, stopping as he stooped over her, his eyes burning into hers.

"Are you telling me you weren't caught by the fire? That you were safely outside but went back in again?"

"Yes." She was not sure what he was driving at. "I heard a horse cry and I couldn't be sure if you had four or five. I'd got out Gilda and the other three and I couldn't bear to let a fifth one die." She shivered. "I definitely heard it."

"Imagination," he said tersely, "or else it was one of the others. In any event it was a damn fool thing to do. Much as I value my bloodstock, I value a human life more. When I think what could have happened to you if I hadn't reached you in time—"

His voice was raw with anger, but she loved every harsh note of it, realising how shocked he was by her narrow escape from death and how much of himself he was unconsciously disclosing.

"How did you find me?" she asked.

"By sheer luck. I was on my way home when I saw smoke on the skyline. I drove like a demon, I can tell you, and reached the stables just as part of the wall collapsed. I caught a glimpse of something blue and—" Adam stopped speaking, his expression clearly showing how real the memory still was for him. "I'm not sure why I knew it was you. But there seemed no doubt of it."

"Maybe you associate me with accidents," she said lightly. "But thank goodness you do. You saved my life."

"I'd like to know who caused the fire," he said grimly. "They rarely start by themselves."

"No one was there," she said, startled.

"There might have been earlier on." He looked at her searchingly and she made an effort to return it.

"I didn't have any assignation there with Simon," she said raggedly. "So if that's what's in your mind, forget it."

"Very well." He walked to the door. "The doctor will be here soon. I'll go and wait for him."

"I don't need a doctor."

Not deigning to reply, he left the room, and Sharon relaxed against the pillow and watched the streaks of daylight searching out the chinks in the curtains. Had she been dreaming, or had Adam really called her darling? He had spoken with such tenderness and fear.

Her thoughts were interrupted by the arrival of the doctor, who quickly established that there was nothing wrong with her that a good rest would not put right.

"If your headache doesn't ease off," he said on his way out, "let me know. You've had a minor concussion and I don't want you going silly on me!"

"You mean sillier!" she smiled, and was still smiling somewhat illogically, when Adam returned.

"You're to stay in bed all day," he pronounced. "I'll tell Mother you have a cold. Don't mention the fire when you do see her."

"I wouldn't dream of it," Sharon said indignantly. "I'm not a fool."

He looked so sardonic that she immediately regretted her reply. How quickly he had reverted to his earlier antagonism now he knew she was unhurt! If receiving his tenderness meant having to be ill, she could see herself becoming a permanent invalid.

"Beryl's bringing you a hot drink," he went on. "If there's anything else you need, ring the bell."

"Yes, sir," she said meekly, which brought her another of his sardonic looks before he departed.

Although she had professed to be unharmed by her experience, Sharon was glad of a day in bed, and she slept for the best part of it. It was late afternoon before she awoke. She felt considerably better and was debating whether Adam would be provoked to further argument if she got dressed, when Beryl came in with a large bunch of yellow roses.

Sharon held out her arms. "How lovely! Are they from—?"

"Mr. Lennox, madam. He heard of your accident and called with them."

"How nice of him!" Sharon strove to keep the disappointment from her voice as she buried her head in the scented blooms. Serve her right for thinking Adam had sent them. She handed them back to Beryl to put in water and then made sure the vase was placed out of her line of vision. The last thing she wanted was to be reminded of Simon.

"Is Mr. Adam in London?" she asked casually.

"Yes. But he didn't leave till late this morning. He waited till you'd had your breakfast." The maid chuckled. "He was pacing the hall when I came down with your empty tray. Reminded me of an expectant father!"

Sharon lowered her head, embarrassed by the warmth

that flooded through her at Beryl's remark. If Adam was anxious about her, he was going to extraordinary lengths not to let her know it. It had to mean he was still fighting his attraction for her—and the only reason he fought it must have been that he still believed the worst of her.

Her impulse to get up for dinner faded. There was no point making an effort to be nice to him. He saw her in a particular light and nothing she did would alter his opinion.

The next morning, fully recovered, she called on Mrs. Peters. The woman was touchingly pleased to see her, though worried that she might have got up too soon.

"You modern girls tend to treat colds too lightly," she warned.

"It was only a slight one," Sharon lied. "Not bad enough for me to have stayed in bed at all, except that Adam insisted."

"Did he really?" His mother looked delighted. "I'm so glad he's taking care of you."

Sharon quickly changed the subject. "You're the important one. How are *you* feeling?"

"Bored."

"Are there any errands I can do for you? Buy some magazines for you to read, perhaps?"

"What a good idea." Mrs. Peters mused quietly for an instant. "If you wouldn't object to taking a bus, you could go into Milwood and change my library books. I'm afraid Adam has the car."

"I'll enjoy a bus ride," Sharon assured her.

"If you stayed on here I'd get you a car of your own," Mrs. Peters said.

Sharon made no comment, and with a sigh her mother-in-law pointed to the two novels on her bedside table.

"The library has my list," she explained, "so make sure Miss Hodges gives you something from it. She's always trying to fob me off with books of her own taste!"

Happy at the chance to be useful—if only in a minor way—Sharon set off for the market town. She had no idea when the buses ran, but since she had all day to waste, it didn't really matter. She also welcomed the opportunity to get away from Green Spinney, and with an almost light heart she reached the bus stop and settled herself for a long wait. The sun shone down on her head and a slight breeze ruffled her silvery hair. A bumblebee droned past and settled on the hedgerow, its buzzing merging into the louder drone of the single-decker red bus she could see grinding its way up the hill.

It drew to a stop in front of her and she took a seat near the door. At this time of the morning there were few people on it: a couple of women with shopping baskets and some children giggling and quarrelling among themselves. In spite of empty roads and few stops, the journey to Milwood took half an hour and Sharon descended at the town centre feeling soothed by the pleasant jogging journey through the countryside.

She strolled down the High Street until she found the library, and though the librarian asserted that she had just the book for Mrs. Peters, Sharon insisted on her finding something from her mother-in-law's list. After completing a couple of errands—a packet of long pins for Beryl and some herbal tea for the cook—she decided to have a cup of coffee. Entering a small chintz-and-bamboo coffee shop, she took a seat near the window. Hardly had she settled down when a man's voice spoke her name and Simon bore down on her.

"What a stroke of luck to see you here," he smiled. "I called at the house this morning to find out how you were and was told you'd gone shopping."

"There was no reason I shouldn't. I'm as fit as a flea!"

He glanced at the chair beside her and she nodded, knowing she had no choice to do otherwise. She remembered their last meeting, but then remembered the yellow roses he had sent her.

"The flowers were lovely," she said.

"It was the least I could do."

His voice was grim and she noticed he had lost some of his ruddy colour. It made him look older than usual and, not for the first time, she wondered why he had never married.

"It was my fault, you know," he burst out.

"The fire?"

"Yes. After you left me the other morning I was so fed up I hardly knew what I was doing. I stabled the horses, but later that night I couldn't remember if I'd bolted the stalls properly. I went back to check—I had shut the doors after all—and then hung around there while I chewed over some of the problems that have been bugging me lately. I was smoking at the time and I guess I dropped the butt and didn't grind it out properly. Adam will fire me when he finds out—which is exactly what *I'd* do if I were him." Simon's face was twisted with anguish. "I could have killed you, Sharon! Do you realise that?"

"But you didn't. I'm perfectly all right, and so are the horses."

"That doesn't lessen my guilt." He banged one hand upon the other. He made no sound, yet the very quietness of the gesture emphasised the fierce emotion inside him. "I don't blame you for sending me away the other morning. In your place I'd have done the same. I behaved like a swine! And then to cause the fire and nearly burn you alive! God, when I think of it—"

"Don't think of it," she soothed. "It's over and no one's been hurt."

"You really mean that, don't you? You've no malice in you at all."

"Why should I have? You didn't set fire to the stables deliberately; it was an accident. And you didn't kiss me to order to harm me, so—"

"I harmed myself," he interjected. "Because now you won't see me."

"We're having coffee together," she pointed out. "I could have said no."

"You mean you—you mean you've changed your mind? You'll still be friends with me?" He went to catch her hand and stopped himself in time. "I won't touch you again, I swear it. Just as long as we're friends—"

Dismayed by his over-reaction, Sharon longed to escape, but was reluctant to do so while he was in such a state of agitation.

"Of course we're friends, Simon. But even friends must part—when it comes to being late for lunch!"

"I'll run you home in the car."

Hiding her reluctance to go with him, she accepted the offer. But once they were alone on the open road her embarrassment died, for Simon was as good as his word and talked only of impersonal things. It was like the first few occasions they had gone out and she had regarded him as a friend. Now he was behaving like one again, though she couldn't bank on his remaining that way. He loved her and was bound to try his luck with her again.

"I'll be seeing you," he said as he dropped her outside her front door. "You know where I am if you need me."

Nodding, she left him, and was crossing the hall when Beryl came out of the dining room.

"Lunch is ready, Mrs. Peters. Will you be long?"

"Just give me time to wash my hands."

Sharon ran up to her room, hurriedly tidied herself and reached the dining-room door as Beryl wheeled in the trolley.

"Cheese soufflé!" she exclaimed. "Oh, good. I adore—" she stopped, discomfited to see Adam seated at the table. "I thought you were in London."

"I don't go every day." He rose and held a chair for her. "How are you today?"

"Back to normal, thanks. The fire seems like a dream."

"A nightmare," he said shortly.

She looked at him and it was then she noticed that his right hand was bandaged. Words trembled on her lips, but she held them back until Beryl had gone out.

"I—I didn't know you'd hurt your hand," she said jerkily "Was it in the fire ?"

"It's nothing. A slight burn."

"It wouldn't be so heavily bandaged for a slight burn."

He shrugged and, picking up his fork in his left hand, began to eat. His gesture was ungainly and tears filled her eyes.

"I'd no—no idea," she stammered. "You must be in dreadful pain."

"Forget it."

His voice was as cold as his expression, and after watching him surreptitiously for a few minutes Sharon, too, began to eat. How controlled he was! How much the master of the situation. Yet he had disregarded his own safety when he thought she was in danger, had recklessly entered a blazing building to save a woman he despised. She swallowed convulsively and put down her fork, restraining a mad impulse to run over and cradle his head in her arms.

"Where were you this morning?" Adam asked abruptly.

"I went to Milwood to change your mother's library books."

"With Simon ?"

"Why, no." She raised her eyebrows. "I met him there by accident."

"How fortuitous!"

"Not particularly." Sensing the anger in him, she made an effort to control her own. "I went to a café for some coffee and he saw me and followed me in."

"And drove you home ?"

"Is there any reason why he shouldn't?"

Adam swallowed hard and she was reminded of the quarrel she had overheard between the two men, when he had practically ordered Simon to tell her the truth about himself. But what truth? To ask Adam would be tantamount to a confession of eavesdropping.

"Simon is a friend of mine," she said stonily. "Unless you can give me a good reason why I shouldn't see him—"

"He has a job to do. It's a strenuous one and should occupy all his time. Making sheep's eyes at you isn't part of it! Anyway, you'll be gone from here in a few weeks. Playing him along will only hurt him unnecessarily."

"Oh, I see now." The truth hit her with a sting that made her wince. "You're not concerned about my hurting Simon; you're worried about your own peace of mind. You're afraid I might decide to accept his proposal and stay on here as his wife. That would really put paid to your attempt to be rid of me." Her voice rose. "I'm surprised you didn't leave me in the stables the other night. If I'd burned to death you'd have been rid of me for good!"

"Shut up!" Fury brought his fork crashing to the table. "I might wish you'd never been born, but I could never wish you dead!"

"You surprise me," she drawled.

"I surprise myself," he said flatly, and pricked up his fork. "Get on with your lunch, Sharon. If you rush from the room in a temper the servants will talk."

"Let them! I don't care."

"But I do. My mother would hear of it and would

want to know why." Grey eyes raked her like knife blades.

"And since you're here in order to keep her happy, I suggest you bear it in mind."

"I'm leaving the minute she's better," Sharon stated.

"By then you will have done what you intended, so there'll be no need for you to stay. And don't stare at me with wounded eyes," he said savagely. "You came here to wheedle your way into her affections and you've succeeded beyond your wildest dreams. You'll be one of her beneficiaries when she dies and—"

"Oh no!" Sharon cried.

"Oh yes," he mocked. "Don't try to look shocked. It's what you've been angling for since you arrived."

She saw the contempt in his face, and the anger she had been trying to control was no longer manageable. She longed to hurt him as he was hurting her, to make him lose his pride and writhe with self-disgust.

"I haven't only wheedled myself into your mother's heart," she said with calculated precision. "I've got into your heart, too. You may make Helen your wife, but it won't stop you wanting me!"

Adam's face became a mask. All expression was washed from it. He closed his eyes momentarily, as if unable to bear the sight of her, and when the lids rose again he was in charge of himself.

"A few more comments like that," he said softly, "and I'll call you Lucy."

"Lucy?" she queried.

"The feminine of Lucifer. You are indeed a fitting wife for the devil!"

CHAPTER NINE

A WARM May gave way to a blazing June, and Mrs. Peters, slow to regain her strength, was more dependent than ever upon a daughter-in-law she was fast regarding as a daughter.

Sharon found the woman's affection both heartwarming and disturbing, for it made her eventual departure seem somehow traitorous. But she could not remain. Even if she wanted to do so, Adam would not countenance it.

Since their bitter quarrel, when she had taunted him with wanting her, they had barely spoken to one another. They met a few evenings a week at dinner, when their conversation was monosyllabic, and he was careful never to be present when she was with his mother, for this would have meant both of them making a pretence at friendship that would have been far too trying.

It was during one of their uneasy silences at dinner that Beryl came in to say there was a telephone call for her.

"Are you sure it's for me and not my mother-in-law?" Sharon asked.

"It's for Mrs. Rufus Peters," Beryl replied, and Sharon hurried out to take the call.

"And about time, too," a sharp feminine voice said.

"I'm sorry to have kept you waiting," Sharon apologised. "I wasn't sure if the call was for me."

"Don't tell me you've forgotten your name?" the

answer came back. "Are you able to come up and see me?"

"Who are you?" Sharon asked.

"Don't give me that! I want to talk to you, and fast."

"Are you sure you have the right Mrs. Peters?"

"The right one—and the wrong one." The voice was even more waspish. "But I'm not saying any more over the telephone. I'm at the Palace Park Hotel in London. Room 304. I'll expect you tomorrow morning."

"I'm not going to London tomorrow," Sharon protested.

"Yes, you are. As early as you can make it. I don't want to wait about all day."

The connection was severed with a sharp click and Sharon stared at the receiver with agitation. Who was the caller, and why had she sounded so venomous? Even more important, what right did she have to issue orders and expect them to be obeyed?

Trembling with anxiety, she returned to the dining room and made a pretence of resuming her meal. She knew Adam was watching her and sensed his curiosity, but for some reason was determined not to satisfy it.

"Is anything wrong?" he asked at last. "You look very pale."

"I—I—" She bit her lip. "I'm fine, thank you."

"Who was it?" he asked.

"I don't know."

His already dark skin took on a darker hue. "You don't need to lie to me, Sharon. If you don't wish me to know, you have merely to say so."

"I didn't think you'd be interested in anyone who knew me," she replied.

"Only if it affects my mother."

"I'll let you know if it does. Until then, don't concern yourself with my affairs."

"Affairs?" he echoed sardonically. "I'm sure that word has special significance for you."

Silently she went on eating, forcing herself to swallow food that now tasted like straw to her.

It was not until she was in her bedroom that she dared to let herself wonder again about her mysterious caller. Why was the woman so hostile? And who was she? No matter how painful the answers to these questions might be, any truth would be better than living in a vacuum.

Anxiously she wondered what excuse she could find for going to London tomorrow. If only there was someone in whom she could confide. Her thoughts flew to Adam and for a moment she remembered the tenderness in his voice the night of the fire. Then she recalled his harshness to her ever since and knew he was the last person she would dare enlist for help.

Simon, perhaps? He would be a sympathetic listener. But no, it would be better to wait until she had discovered the identity of her caller and found out what she wanted.

It was while she was chatting to her mother-in-law before the nurse settled her for the night that she was given an excuse to go to London.

"Your hair has grown so long," Mrs Peters exclaimed, "that the style Gerald gave you is completely lost."

"Perhaps I'll go and see him tomorrow."

"That's a good idea. And buy yourself some pretty dresses at the same time."

"I don't need any more clothes," Sharon protested. "The hairdresser will be quite enough expense."

The following morning she awoke at seven, snatched a hurried cup of coffee in the kitchen and was ringing for a taxi when Adam came down the stairs.

"Where are you going at this hour?" he asked.

"To London. Your mother wants me to have my hair done."

"Indeed? Are you sure your trip isn't connected with your telephone call last night?"

She did not answer and he took the receiver from her hand and replaced it on the cradle. "You don't need the train. You can come up with me in the car."

"I'd prefer to go by train," she said coldly.

"I'd prefer it if you did, too. But since everyone here knows I go to London on Fridays, it will look strange if you don't come with me."

Knowing it was useless to argue, she followed him to the car. The chauffeur was driving them, she saw gratefully, so she would at least be spared Adam's insults, if not his company.

Adam buried himself in a newspaper and Sharon unbuttoned the jacket of her silk two-piece suit and moved nearer to the window. Tentatively she lowered it, waiting for a reprimand from the man beside her. But none came, and she lowered the window a fraction more and allowed a cooling breeze to lift the silky strands of her hair. Carelessly she pushed them behind her ears, all at once conscious of Adam dropping his paper and looking at her.

"In profile you don't look more than seventeen," he commented. "What do you intend to do with your life when you leave here?"

"I don't know. What do you suggest?"

"Find something worthwhile to do."

"Good works instead of naughty play!" It was impossible for her not to laugh. "Honestly, you don't wear blinkers as far as I'm concerned; you're just plain blind!"

Her laughter stopped abruptly and she turned away to hide her tears. How could Adam think her as wicked as he did? Didn't men have any intuition, or did facts, once presented, become sacrosanct?

The car purred along smoothly and it was some time before he spoke again, his voice so reflective that she almost felt he was unaware he was giving utterance to his thoughts.

"If I were the sort of person who could fool myself, I might be able to find some happiness. Lord knows I've wanted a family of my own for long enough. But I've never been able to settle for second best."

"Perhaps you're looking for a saint, not a woman. No one is perfect."

"I realize that. But where does one draw the line?" He rested his head against the seat, ruffling the silky black hair that lay sleek against his neck.

"I don't think there can be a line, Adam. If you love someone, you do so regardless of their faults."

"I thought you were going to say because of them!"

"You might overlook them," she said wryly, "but you couldn't pretend they weren't there!"

"Could you?"

"If I loved someone I doubt if I'd see their faults."

"Spoken like a true woman," he mocked. "Though I refuse to believe you were blind to Rufus's."

"I can't imagine myself married to a man who drank and gambled," she said abruptly.

"Can't you?"

He paused, as if waiting for her to say more, and when she didn't, he sighed heavily, his well-shaped eyebrows meeting above his nose in a frown.

"I've never met anyone whose looks were so deceptive. Fair of face and—Damn you!" he exclaimed in anguish. "Why did you have to come into my life? I was almost beginning to think I'd found what I was looking for."

"In Helen?" she questioned, goaded into self-defence, though she was quite sure what it was she was defending. A good name she appeared not to have? A heart he had already broken in two?

"In Helen," he agreed. "I know you don't like her, but—"

"That's not true," Sharon said coldly. "I'm indifferent to her. It's she who doesn't like me."

"Because you married Rufus."

"Not true," Sharon said again, boldly adding, "It's because I'm beautiful and she's afraid you'll notice it."

"I'd have to be blind not to," he said, and suddenly he pulled her forward until she was in his arms. At once his mouth came down on hers. It was warm and firm and drew a response from her she was powerless to deny. Her lips parted and she pressed closer to him, uncaring of anything except his nearness. With a strangled murmur he pushed her away, his quick glance at the chauffeur's solid back indicating one reason, though his words gave her another.

"It's no use, Sharon. My oblivion would only be temporary. Passion doesn't last for ever."

"Thanks for your honesty!" she said drily.

"Would you rather I wasn't?"

She shook her head and huddled back in the corner, as far away from him as possible. They finished the rest of the drive in silence, and it was only when they reached Marble Arch in London that she spoke.

"I'll get out here if you don't mind."

"We can drop you at the hairdresser's."

"No, thanks."

Telling the chauffeur to stop, Adam scribbled something on a piece of paper and handed it to her. "Here's where I'll be. Give me a call and let me know where I can pick you up. I'll be ready any time after five."

Putting the paper in her handbag, she stepped out of the car, waiting until it had disappeared into the stream of traffic before turning into Park Lane and heading for the Palace Park Hotel. Taking the lift to the third floor, she soon found herself standing outside room 304. Her heart was beating an uneven tattoo, but afraid to wait until it steadied—in case she turned tail and fled—she tapped on the door. Almost immediately it was opened by a tall, thin woman in her early thirties. She wore a modish linen dress and her face was vividly made up.

Her hair was the same colour as Sharon's, but palpably dyed and set in an elaborate style.

"So you finally came." The woman motioned her to enter and added, "I expected you an hour ago."

"I live a long way from London," Sharon explained, "and I came up by car."

"Good for you!" the woman said sarcastically. "You might as well make the most of your good life; it won't last long." She took a cigarette from a box, sat in an armchair and crossed one leg over the other. "Well, what do you have to tell me?"

Sharon stood by the window.

"I'm afraid I don't understand. You'll have to explain yourself. You see, I was in a plane crash and—"

"I know all about that," the woman interrupted. "But you look fine to me. So quit the stall and answer my question. What's been happening?"

"At Green Spinney?"

"I don't mean Buckingham Palace! Tell me how you're doing. Is the old girl fond of you yet?"

There was an avid curiosity on the over-painted face that made Sharon reluctant to satisfy it.

"I don't see what business it is of yours. If you won't tell me who you are—"

She moved to the door, but found her way barred.

"Don't give me that! You know damn well who I am."

Sharon looked at her coldly. Now that she was face to face with her telephone caller, her fear had gone and she felt only dislike.

"I've lost my memory," she stated. "I don't remember anything that happened before the plane crash."

"So that's it," the woman muttered, her hard blue eyes searching Sharon's face. As though satisfied with what they saw there, she relaxed. "I guess you're telling the truth. Your face was always a giveaway. Don't you remember anything?"

"No, I was hoping you could help me. Naturally I've learned a lot from my in-laws."

"I'll bet!"

"Do you know them?"

"Only by repute. And enough to stay well out of their way."

Sharon went on studying her companion. She could not imagine having anything in common with her, yet obviously they had been closely acquainted in the past.

She took a deep breath. "Would you mind telling me who you are?" she asked.

"Sharon Peters."

"*What?*"

The woman laughed. "You heard me. I'm Sharon Peters."

"You can't be!"

"I am. You're Sharon Moore. It was our having the same Christian name that gave me the idea in the first place."

"I can't even begin to follow you." Shakily Sharon collapsed on to the nearest chair. "If you could explain things from the beginning," she pleaded.

The woman shrugged and lit another cigarette.

"I married Rufus in Cape Town and he moved into my place and decided not to go back to his uncle's farm."

"That much I know," said Sharon. "Adam told me."

"I daresay. And a pretty sour version of it, too, if I know anything about him. His letters were always cold as icebergs. What else has he told you about my marriage?"

"That his brother wasn't happy with you and that you were unfaithful to him," Sharon said bluntly.

"How charming!" The woman looked bitter. "What else did he say? I'm sure there was more than that."

"He said you encouraged Rufus to drink and gamble."

"That's a good one! As if Rufus ever needed any encouragement!" His widow inhaled on her cigarette and blew out an unhealthy cloud of smoke. "The one thing I could never stand about Adam was the way he kidded himself about Rufus. He'd never admit his brother was a no-good with or without me! Anyway, if he'd come across with the money we wanted, I'd have made Rufus a good wife. I wanted to settle in London, but Adam swore he wouldn't give us a penny if we did. It was stupid of him to show his hand that way, because I used it as a lever. Adam was willing to pay us anything to prevent his mother from finding out what we were like—or rather what I was like."

"But Adam never knew you," protested Sharon.

"Rufus wrote him plenty." The dyed blonde head wagged. "I couldn't care less what he said about me as long as the money kept coming. But when Rufus was killed, Adam refused to send another cent."

"Because Rufus had already left you."

"I was still his legal wife when he copped it."

The woman—it was difficult for Sharon to think of her as Mrs. Peters—stood up and angrily paced the room.

"I'd no intention of being left high and dry financially and I wrote to Adam and told him so. I warned him I'd hotfoot it to England unless he put his hand in his pocket, and after a lot of argy-bargy he came up with five thousand pounds and the offer of an allowance—as long as I kept away from his mother. Then out of the blue I got a letter from the old girl herself. Lord knows how she found my address, but—"

"Adam left the envelope lying on his desk," Sharon explained.

The woman gave a peal of laughter.

"What a gas! Serve him right. Anyway, the old girl begged me to come and stay with her said she was longing to meet her darling Rufus's widow. I wrote back saying I was broke and she sent an air ticket by return." There was a pause. "That's where you came in."

Sharon's heart began to pound. "How?"

"I should have thought it obvious." The woman studied her appraisingly. "There's one thing you can say for me: I know my limitations. I couldn't see Mrs. Peters taking me to her bosom any more than I could see myself enjoying being clasped there. Apart from which I didn't want to leave Cape Town just then. So I asked you to impersonate me."

"And I agreed?"

"You're here, aren't you?"

"I can't believe it!"

"You were getting well paid."

Sharon swallowed. "You mean I did it for money?"

The real Sharon Peters laughed. "You certainly aren't

doing it for love! One thousand pounds, to be precise."

Sharon was too shocked to speak. She had always refused to agree with Adam's sour view of her, but now this woman was adding to the sourness.

"I don't believe it," she stated with more conviction than she felt. "I wouldn't do a thing like that just for money. I'm not—I don't—I'm not like that," she concluded. "I feel it in my bones."

"Then rattle your bones and try to feel a bit more," came the retort. "You did it for the money, so stop looking so snooty. Though to be fair to you, you wanted the money for your music. Do you remember that you play the piano?" She saw Sharon nod and went on, "You needed the money to continue your studies. That's why you agreed to stay at Green Spinney for a month. The idea was for you to wangle yourself into my mother-in-law's good books and make sure she put you in her will—or rather me—and also get Adam to increase my allowance."

Sharon backed away to the window. "I must have been mad to have agreed. No money in the world would have made me do such a thing."

"Well, you did agree," came the blunt reminder. "For a thousand pounds. And you're going to keep your promise."

"I won't!"

"You have no choice. I can make things awkward for anyone who goes around impersonating me."

"I couldn't have done it without your knowledge," Sharon pointed out.

"I'll say I was ill in a nursing home and that's when

you got the idea of taking my place. A friend of mine runs one and she'll be happy to say I was an inmate." The scarlet-painted mouth curled in a smile. "Shall I go on?"

"No!"

"Just one more thing. If you stay at the Peters's until you've done what you promised, I'll give you five hundred pounds more than we agreed."

"I don't want the money. None of it!"

"That's up to you. But you're going to keep the promise you made to me. If you don't, I'll pay the family a visit myself. I've a couple of weeks to spare and I wouldn't mind playing the sad little widow for a short time."

"You mustn't! Mrs. Peters is ill. The shock of knowing I was an impostor and then meeting you— She'd see through you quicker than you think."

"I'll only do it if you go back on your word," Sharon Peters said placidly.

"If I go through with it, what happens when I leave Green Spinney?"

"When you leave—which, let me remind you, can't be till you've got what I want—you can do what you like. I'll go back to Cape Town and write a monthly letter of love and affection that should keep everyone happy."

Sharon clenched her hands. "It's awful! I can't bear to think of it."

"Then you're stupid. You'll be better off by fifteen hundred pounds and the old girl will have sweet memories of dear Rufus's wife."

Sharon stared at the heavily made-up face. "I still don't believe I did it for the money."

"Why not? You're no better than me, so wipe that haughty look off your face. I'll expect to hear you've completed your side of the bargain within the next two weeks."

Once more in Park Lane, Sharon walked aimlessly. People jostled her, but she neither saw nor felt them. At last she knew the truth about herself, and she wished with all her heart that she was still in ignorance of it. Although she was not the real Sharon Peters and had never behaved as badly as Adam believed, she seemed little better than the hard-faced blonde she had just left. She shuddered. No matter how much her musical career meant to her, how could she have agreed to deceive a dead man's family?

But she had and, because of Mrs. Peters's recent heart attack, was forced to continue with the deception. If she didn't the real Sharon would have no compunction about going to Green Spinney and telling her mother-in-law the truth about Rufus.

I'll leave the moment Mrs. Peters has recovered, she vowed. Then I'll tell Adam the truth and let him deal with his sister-in-law any way he likes.

It was not a solution that pleased her, for it meant further pretence on her part, but it was the only one she could think of. In a few weeks, if things went well, she would be free to leave Green Spinney and Adam. Most of all Adam—from whom she would never truly be free.

CHAPTER TEN

UNABLE to face the meaningless trivia of a two-hour session at a Mayfair hairdresser, Sharon decided to return home. Home, she thought bitterly, knowing that Green Spinney could never be this to her.

It was only when her train was already pulling out of the station that she realised she had forgotten to call Adam. Still, as he disliked her so much, giving him another reason to do so would hardly make any difference.

As soon as she reached the house she went to see her mother-in-law. But no, she mustn't think of her as that. Mrs. Peters was a stranger and the sooner she became so in actuality, the better.

"You're back early, my dear." The old lady was reading a newspaper, but put it aside happily as Sharon came toward her.

"Gerald couldn't fit me in. I should have booked an appointment."

"I've never known him refuse before. I'll phone him and—"

"Please don't. It wasn't his fault. He had so many customers that he couldn't have squeezed me in. Actually I didn't even ask him."

With distaste, Sharon wondered if her life of deceit had turned her into a first-class liar. Never had she believed that falsehoods could roll so glibly off her tongue.

"Why didn't you let someone else do your hair?" asked Mrs Peters. "I wanted you to look pretty tonight."

"Why tonight?"

"Didn't Adam tell you? You're dining at Helen's."

"He never said a word," said Sharon.

"Isn't that just like him? He took it for granted you'd go, I suppose. What will you wear?"

Sharon forced herself to think about it. "My blue silk."

"Why not the lilac? You haven't worn it once.'

"I've hardly worn any of the things you bought me. You were much too extravagant." How the real Sharon Peters would despise her for saying such a thing!

"Nonsense," the older woman said. "I enjoy spending money on you. It's one of the few pleasures I have."

"I'm not sure Adam likes it."

"He has no reason to worry," was the firm answer. "He is head of the company and very successful."

"What does he do?" Uttering the question made Sharon realize how little she knew about him.

"I suppose one could call him a business entrepreneur," his mother replied. "He dabbles in lots of things: engineering, property, farming. He's a highly eligible man, you know. I only wish he'd hurry up and marry. Then if I could persuade you to stay with me permanently, I'd have the two things I want most in the world."

Too moved to speak, Sharon silently pressed Mrs. Peters's hand.

"You bring Rufus so close to me," the woman went on. "If only you had had a child." Sharon pulled her hand away and Mrs. Peters stopped abruptly. "Forgive me, my dear. I shouldn't have said that. You're young and beautiful and you can't spend the rest of your life mourning for Rufus. I don't blame you for wanting to leave here. It's wrong of me to keep reminding you of things you're trying to forget."

"That isn't the reason," Sharon said hastily. "Please don't stop talking of Rufus if it makes you happy. It's just that I'm not sure it's good for you to keep harking back to the past."

"Perhaps I won't when I've other things to look forward to."

A small silver clock chimed the hour and Mrs. Peters frowned. "Time's getting on. You'd better go and do your hair. And be sure to come in and see me before you leave."

The prospect of dining with Helen was not something Sharon relished, particularly that night, when all she wanted was to be left alone to think over everything that had happened. But having failed Adam once today she was unwilling to incur his wrath again.

The knowledge that she was not Rufus's wife—not anyone's wife, in fact—made her feel more her own person. Before, she had a reputation to live up to. Now, she had a sense of freedom, which she marked by wearing her hair differently—long and loose—and by choosing the least sophisticated dress in her wardrobe. It was in cream Indian cotton with a tucked bodice, and square neck and long sleeves.

As soon as she was dressed, she paid her promised visit to Mrs. Peters, whose expression told her she had never looked lovelier, then went downstairs in search of Adam. She found him in the drawing-room, his manner aloof as he regarded her.

"Why didn't you have the courtesy to call and let me know you weren't coming back with me from London?" he asked.

She clutched her handbag tightly. "I forgot. When I remembered, I was already on the train."

"You could have phoned me when you got home."

"It was too late."

"It's never too late for good manners. Or was your appointment in town so important that you forgot everything else?"

"The hairdresser couldn't take me," she lied.

"I wasn't referring to the hairdresser," he said, "but to the rendezvous you made with your telephone caller last night."

Her cheeks flamed, giving her away, and his expression became harder. "I assumed it was with someone you knew in South Africa?"

"Yes."

"A man?"

"No," she replied, and looked away.

"I don't believe you," he said harshly. "But keep it a secret if you wish. I don't care what you do when you're away from here, as long as you behave yourself while you're in my home."

Stung, she turned on him. "You could do with a few lessons on how to behave, too! You might at least have told me I was invited to Helen's tonight, instead of taking it for granted I'd come."

"I overlooked it," he said stiffly. "It won't happen again." He stared at his watch. "We'd better go."

Silently Sharon followed him to the car, dismayed to see he was going to do the driving. If he used the journey to berate her further, she'd get out and walk!

"You look different tonight," he remarked as he set the car in motion.

"My hair's longer."

"And your neckline is higher." His tone was dry. "Have you decided to play the ingénue?"

"I thought you'd find it less disturbing!" she said coldly.

"It isn't what shows that counts. A cover-up can sometimes be more revealing. Which reminds me, you'll be meeting several of our close neighbours and friends this evening, so watch yourself."

Abruptly she was possessed by such a wild longing to tell him the truth about herself—or the little she knew of it—that she started to tremble.

She was still trembling when they reached the large Queen Anne house set back at the end of an uneven lane. The front door was open and they walked through the hall into a rectangular drawing-room. It was crowded with people and Helen disengaged herself from a group by the window and crossed to meet them. In black silk, with diamonds at her throat, she looked every inch the grande dame.

"How late you are! We've been holding dinner for you." She slipped her arm through Adam's and drew him away. He moved a step, then stopped and spoke to Sharon.

"Come along, I'll introduce you to some of our neighbours."

"How sweet of you to play host," Helen said with a smile.

"It's the least I can do," he answered, flinging Helen a sardonic look that the woman met with a shrug.

With the ease of familiarity, Adam escorted Sharon around the room, and she was soon lost in a welter of names and faces. Finally everyone moved into the dining-room, and Sharon found herself seated next to an elderly gentleman named Colonel Gerard. Hearing that she came from South Africa he bored her with a long story of the Boer War, and she was hard put to it to listen with a semblance of attention. Farther down the table she noticed Simon, who raised his eyebrows as he glanced from her to the Colonel.

After dinner he made an attempt to join her, but was skilfully manoeuvred away by Helen, who had placed Sharon next to a middle-aged vicar and his wife, a friendly but dull couple who discoursed endlessly on child welfare.

Adam was fully preoccupied with Helen, who was as possessive of him as if he were already her husband. More so, Sharon thought bitterly, for as a husband he might have been allowed to circulate among the guests and not be expected to act as a permanent armrest. Stonily she watched him, wishing her bones did not seem to turn to jelly each time he casually glanced in her direction. He was the most handsome man in the room, with his wide-shouldered grace and shining black head.

Finally, pleading a need for fresh air, she managed to disengage herself from her companions and wandered out into the garden. A large oak tree stood guard by a small pool, and she paused under its branches and listened to the hooting of an owl.

"You look like the sugar-plum fairy standing there." A male voice spoke out of the darkness. "Is your hair real or is it candy-floss?"

She turned and saw a smiling young man. "It's candy-floss. It melts in the sunshine."

"Then this is certainly not ill met by moonlight, Titania! You're Adam's sister-in-law, aren't you? I'm Tony Gerard, one of your neighbours when I'm not in London. You met my father earlier on."

"Oh!" Sharon exclaimed.

"You may well say 'oh'. Most people say 'ouch'!"

"That's not a very filial thing to say!" commented Sharon.

"Only a filial would dare say it!" He grinned. "I'd knock down anyone else who did!"

She laughed. "I know much more about the Boer War now."

"I'd rather you knew more about me. I'd certainly like to know about you. I can't think why Helen didn't put me next to you tonight."

"Perhaps she thought I'd find your father more amusing!"

"Oh dear, you're not a fairy after all. Just a pussycat." He held out his arms. "Would you care to dance with me?"

"Here?" she queried.

"And now!"

Smiling, Sharon stepped closer and he started to sing and waltz her over the lawn. Her skirts billowed out as they twirled round and round.

"You're as light as a blossom," he whispered. "What's your name?"

"Sharon."

"A beautiful name for a beautiful girl."

He swung her to a stop and, as he did, she saw Adam and Helen come through the French windows.

"We have an audience," she murmured. The young man looked behind him.

"Hi!" he called. "Come and join the party."

"The party's up here," Helen drawled. "But we don't mind if you'd rather be alone."

Sharon pulled away from Tony's arm and moved toward the house, conscious of Adam's stony gaze. "I was getting a breath of air. It was hot inside."

"You'll hardly cool off by cavorting around the lawn." Helen sounded amused.

"We weren't cavorting," said Tony. "We were dancing on a cloud." He touched Sharon's silver-blonde hair. "Let's go in and play two-handed bridge; then no one can make nasty remarks!"

"It's time we were leaving," Adam interposed.

"Just my luck!" Tony said, still looking at Sharon. "May I call you during the weekend?"

She hesitated and Helen laughed. "Why ask the obvious, Tony? Sharon will be delighted for you to call her."

"Thanks for answering for me, Helen." Anger

tightened Sharon's voice. "When I want a personal secretary I'll know who to ask."

"I'm not open to offers," Helen drawled.

"I thought you were!"

Tony smothered a laugh and Sharon walked towards the house. She was by the French window when Helen called her.

"By the way, I saw you coming out of the Palace Park Hotel today. But you were so preoccupied you didn't see me." She paused and, when Sharon said nothing, said with amusement, "I hope I haven't said something I shouldn't?"

"Not at all, I was only visiting one of my lovers!"

This time Tony's laugh was loud and, on its echo, Sharon went inside to collect her wrap. She was waiting in the car when Adam came out.

"You might have said good night to the other guests," he said. "It was rude to leave without a word."

"Blame your lady love. She's the one who's rude."

He did not reply and they drove a little way in silence.

"You made a conquest of Tony," he said at last. "What do you think of him?"

"He's charming."

"Nicer than Simon?"

"They're different," she shrugged.

"Don't try and play one off against the other."

"Which one would you prefer me to play with?" she asked. As she noticed his hands clenching on the wheel, she knew a thrill of triumph.

"Neither. All I want is for you to leave here."

"And to leave you in peace."

"I'll never know that any more," he grated. "You've successfully destroyed any hopes I had of—"

She waited, longing for him to see her as she was today and not as he believed her to have been. Yet was Sharon Moore any better than Sharon Peters? The difference lay only in degree, she thought ruefully; the difference between one thousand pounds and several.

"Don't you believe people can change?" she asked huskily.

"Only to a limited extent."

"But some people change entirely. After they've had a traumatic shock or—a religious experience."

"Maybe that does happen," he shrugged. "But I've never seen it for myself. And if you're trying to make me believe you're different from when you arrived here—" He paused. "You've one way to prove it."

"How?"

"If you can ask that, you've only proved my belief. All that's changed about you is your hairstyle!"

Sharon moistened her lips. Her conscience urged her to tell him the truth, tell him and put herself at his mercy. She stole a glance at him and, seeing his firm jaw and strong neck, his narrowed eyes and tightly controlled mouth, knew she could not expect any clemency. Yet in this moment she also knew she could not follow Sharon Peters's wicked plan. She would leave Green Spinney tomorrow, the moment Adam had left the house. But she would also leave him a letter telling him the whole story and where he could contact his real sister-in-law.

"When I—when I go away," she stammered, "I

h-hope you won't think too badly of me. I'm not a very nice person, but I—I could never be as despicable as you think I am."

"At least we're progressing," he said calmly. "For the first time you admit you're not a nice person. Care to confess a bit more?"

His sarcasm completely destroyed the last shreds of any thoughts she had of telling him the truth rather than writing it, and when she answered, her voice was bleak. "The list is far too long to recite. When I've left Green Spinney I'll write you a letter."

"I always knew you—"

But what Adam knew was never disclosed, for just then Green Spinney came in sight, and the lights blazing from the house indicated that something was wrong. In a burst of speed they reached the front door. Adam was the first out of the car, and he raced up to Beryl, who was running towards him.

"I tried to reach you at Miss Helen's, but you'd already left," she said breathlessly.

"Mother?" he said.

"Yes. Nurse has already called the doctor."

With swift strides Adam made for the stairs, Sharon close on his heels. Outside the door of his mother's room he paused, then quietly tapped on the door, pausing again as the nurse appeared.

"It's a gastric attack," she said quietly. "I'd rather you didn't see her until the doctor has seen her."

"Tell her I'm here," said Adam. "Knowing I'm in the house will comfort her."

The nurse nodded and closed the door, and Sharon,

not waiting to see what Adam did, hurried to her own room. It was impossible for her to leave Green Spinney now. Until Mrs. Peters had recovered—or died—she was trapped.

CHAPTER ELEVEN

An hour later Beryl knocked on Sharon's door and told her Adam wished to see her in the library,

"Now?"

"Yes. The doctor's just left."

Smoothing her hair, Sharon sped downstairs. Adam was standing beside the mantelpiece, drumming his fingers on its marble top.

"Your mother?" she asked breathlessly.

"She's holding her own. Apparently there's a virus going around, and in her weakened state—"

"Is there anything I can do?"

"There is!" Unexpectedly he stepped closer to her. "You can give me your word you won't leave here until she's fully recovered."

"Do you need my word for that? Don't you know I wouldn't do anything to hurt her?"

For a moment his eyes roved over her face, as though trying to probe it, then he nodded and stepped back.

"It's just that the way you spoke in the car gave me the impression you were leaving."

"Your impression was right," she said, turning to the door. "But not now. Now I'll stay."

In her room again she undressed and, stretching out on the bed, stared into the darkness. Sharon Peters had given her two weeks to fulfil her side of the bargain. If she didn't, the woman would come here. Of course, she could let the woman know she was already named in Mrs. Peters's will Adam had affirmed this – but the second part of what had to be done – getting a bigger allowance from him – was something that as yet had to be asked for. The ignominy of doing this brought a wave of shame rushing over her. If only she could leave Green Spinney before the end of the two weeks!

The next morning Mrs. Peters had rallied sufficiently for Sharon to visit her, and though she looked frail, she managed her usual perky smile.

"I can only stay a few minutes, darling," Sharon said, bending to kiss her. "You need lots of rest today, but I'll come in and see you again tonight."

"I hope you won't be bored being left so much to yourself. I'm afraid I'll wake up one morning and find you've gone.'

"Not without saying a very long goodbye!" Sharon chided. "You've made me far too comfortable here."

"This is your home, child. You know that."

If only it was, Sharon thought as she went downstairs for breakfast. Adam had already left the house and for the rest of the day she would be on her own.

At lunchtime Tony rang to ask her to have dinner with him that evening, but she refused, giving her mother-in-law's illness as the excuse. As she replaced the telephone she half regretted turning him down. After all, she was not doing any good hanging about the house. However, it was too late to change her mind and she returned to the dining room.

At tea time Simon called by for a short while. He was as sympathetic as always and Sharon nearly confided her problems to him. Yet if she did she would be establishing an intimacy between them that he might easily misconstrue and, for this reason more than any other, she kept her own counsel.

Adam returned while Simon was still talking to her and abruptly called him into the library to discuss some new boundary on the other side of the copse. She did not see Simon again before he left and, hearing his car drive away, took refuge in her room. But she could not hide there the entire evening, and she was forced to dine with Adam and make an effort at conversation. Both were careful not to say anything controversial, and when the meal was over, his relief appeared as heartfelt as her own.

By the end of the week Mrs. Peters had made a marked improvement and Sharon felt free to leave the house for longer and longer intervals. Sometimes she went walking with Sandy, but mostly she went with Simon, accompanying him on his visits to the various farms on the estate. Of Adam she saw little. He drove to London more frequently and would often return after dinner, giving the impression that had it not been for his mother's condition, he would not have returned at all.

One morning, two weeks after Helen's dinner party, Sharon went to Mrs. Peters's room and found her walking around.

"Dr. Matthews says I'm so much better he's going to let me get up for a little while today!" she announced.

"How marvellous!" Sharon was delighted. "That means you'll soon be downstairs and bossing us all again."

"I can't wait! I told you I was tougher than I looked, didn't I? It won't be long before we'll be going on a shopping expedition again."

No words could more clearly have reminded Sharon that her own days there were numbered. It was a painful realisation, for with each passing week she had grown to feel more at home here and more deeply in love with Adam. His dark good looks filled her mind, waking and sleeping, and she knew that never to see him again would leave an emptiness in her life that no one else would be able to fill. If only she dared believe he would forgive her when he learned her true identity! But to hope this was to misunderstand his character. He had such a rigid sense of right and wrong that he would never condone her conduct. Indeed, she could not condone it herself.

The telephone shrilled and she stared at it with loathing, afraid it was the call she was dreading. Sharon Peters must becoming restless and would, without doubt, come here unless she was forestalled.

But luckily it was Simon, and she felt a sense of reprieve that her greeting bordered on effusion.

"Of course, I'd love to go on a picnic," she said. "But give me time to get it organised."

"I've already done it. I've a hamper packed, the car polished and the day free. I'll pick you up in twenty minutes."

Sitting in Simon's sports car a little while later, the countryside unwinding in front of them, Sharon was affected by the high spirits of the man next to her and felt more carefree than she had for some time. How kind he had been to her when she had most needed kindness;

how patient when most men would long since have turned their attention to more affectionate sources.

"Penny for your thoughts," he said. "You've been silent so long they must be worth at least that!"

"I was thinking how nice you are," she said impulsively.

"I told you I grow on people!" he joked. "Next thing you know you'll be thinking me handsome."

Soon they turned off the main road and drove down a narrow country lane. The branches of the trees on both sides formed an archway, darkening the day to green shadow. But ahead it glowed bright again, as if they were being heralded to another world.

"Where are we going?" she asked.

"Wait and see."

He nosed the car into an opening in the hedgerow, stopped it and helped her to alight.

"We'll have to walk the rest of the way," he announced. "But you'll find it's worth it."

She followed him over a stile, across a field and into a wood. Skirting a stream, they walked through an enchanting forest glade and emerged into a bower of green bordered by slender birches. The air was so still and heavy it was almost tangible, and except for the occasional twittering of a bird, the silence was complete.

"It's heavenly!" she exclaimed. "I bet it's where Oberon found Titania asleep."

"You know your Shakespeare," he teased.

"Not only the popular plays. I'm well up on the Tragedies, too." She stopped and frowned. "Now how did I know that?"

"Your memory's coming back. One day you'll remember everything."

Soberly she sat down and he flopped beside her. For a while they lay staring upward at the brilliant blue of the sky. A bee buzzed near her ear, but she was too lazy to move and presently it flew away.

She sat up and looked at Simon. His steady breathing told her he was asleep, and quietly slipping off her sandals, she wandered down the bank to the stream. The water lapped her toes and she shivered with delight.

"Hey there! Fancy sneaking off like that!"

Glancing up, she saw Simon pulling off his shoes and socks. Within a minute they were both wading up and down like a couple of children.

"I don't know about you," he said at last, "but this has given me an appetite for lunch."

"Me, too."

Hand in hand they returned to the glade, where Sharon unpacked the hamper—chicken, salad, tongue, and small individual apple pies—while Simon cooled two cans of beer in the stream. When they finished eating they strolled through the wood, enjoying its green coolness, and it was only as they retraced their steps that Simon caught her by the arm and turned her to face him.

"I want to talk to you, Sharon. I can't go on pretending to be friends when I love you so much. You know how I feel and—"

"You know how I feel," she interrupted. "And I haven't changed."

"You won't let yourself. You're afraid of being hurt again."

"Again ?" she queried.

"You couldn't have been happy with Rufus. Adam may have been blind to his brother's faults, but I wasn't. Rufus couldn't keep any woman happy for long. That's why you're afraid of me. You don't want to make another mistake."

"You couldn't be more wrong !"

She almost told him the truth, held back only by a reluctance she couldn't define, as if she didn't want him to know something that Adam didn't.

"I love you," Simon repeated, "and I want to marry you. If only you'd give yourself a chance to care for me, I know I could make you happy."

Her lips formed the word "no'" and then stopped. Perhaps marriage to Simon was the solution to her problems. He loved her and she was fond of him; in time she might even come to love him, and at least if she became his wife her future would be assured. If she left Green Spinney she would have nowhere to go and, unless her memory returned, she would live the rest of her life in limbo. With Simon as her husband it would not matter if her past remained a blank.

"I don't know what to say," she murmured. "There's so much about myself I don't know. You'd have to take me on trust. I may have done some awful things in the past."

"I'd trust you with my life," he said huskily. "And my past hasn't been blameless, either."

Instantly she remembered the conversation she had overheard between him and Adam.

"You don't need to tell me anything if you don't want to," she whispered. "I'll take you on trust, too."

"Darling."

He drew her head down to rest on his shoulder. He sensed she didn't wish to be kissed and contented himself with stroking her hair and whispering endearments.

"I have so many things to tell you, Sharon, but I don't want to spoil this moment. Let's not think about anything except us."

It was dusk when he left her at Green Spinney, promising to call her later.

"I need time to think," she pleaded. "I haven't made up my mind."

"Let me make your decisions. Rely on me, Sharon."

With a shake of her head, she entered the house. She was halfway up the stairs when Adam came out of the library and called her.

"You're late," he said curtly. "Mother's been asking for you."

"Simon and I went on a picnic," she explained.

"Still playing around with him!" he exclaimed. "Won't you ever learn?"

"Learn what? That I should obey you when you order me to stop seeing him?"

"Don't you know it's for your own good?"

"You don't give a damn about my good! If you did, you wouldn't be so anxious to get rid of me."

"Do you suggest I keep you here permanently?"

His question reminded her she was not what she pretended, and her anger abated. But her hurt remained and, determined not to let him guess it, she said, "I don't want you to interfere in my life. I may marry Simon and I'd rather you didn't say anything about him that you'll regret."

"All I regret is that I haven't said a few things about him before." Adam was so pale with anger that his tanned skin was robbed of warmth. "Though why I should care if you're cited in a divorce case is beyond me. Maybe you'd enjoy seeing your picture in the tabloids."

"What divorce case?" she asked.

"The one Jane will bring when she finds out about you."

"Why should his sister—"

"*Sister?*—" Adam barked. Then he laughed. "So that's what he's told you? Well, I'm sorry to shatter your illusions—though I guess they deserve to be shattered—but Jane happens to be his wife."

Sharon clutched the banister and stared at Adam in horror. "You're lying."

"Ask him yourself. I told him weeks ago to tell you, but he didn't have the guts."

"So you told me instead. I'm surprised you bothered. Think what a laugh you'd have had if I'd—" her breath caught on the words, "If I'd married him bigamously."

"Simon wouldn't do that," Adam answered quietly. "But he might have involved you in a messy court case. And contrary to what you think, I don't want that to happen to you."

"Naturally." Her voice was like ice. "It would break your mother's heart."

There was another flash of anger in his eyes, as if she

had said something to arouse it again. But when he spoke, no anger was apparent.

"I'm not your enemy, Sharon. If things were different, if you had—" He shrugged. "I'm sure Simon would have told you about Jane. It was wrong of me to do it for him. But you made me lose my temper."

"It doesn't matter. It's put things into perspective for me."

"In what way?"

"I wasn't completely convinced it was right to marry him. Now I know it isn't." Her desire to hurt the man in front of her spurred her on. "With a bigger allowance from you and a nest-egg to look forward to from your mother, why should I bother with the problem of a husband!"

"Why, you—"

Not waiting to hear the completion of his sentence, Sharon turned and fled.

CHAPTER TWELVE

NOT until she was soaking in a warm bath was Sharon able to absorb all she had learned about Simon. But she could not think harshly of him. His deception had been motivated by his love for her, but the deception she'd practised had been motivated solely by gain.

She stepped out of her bath and, reaching for a towel, saw herself in the mirror. The roundness of her hips, the curves of her shoulders and the swell of her firm breasts told her she was beautiful. But it was a beauty she would never be able to give to Simon, nor to any other man except one. It was a decision she would have reached in her own good time, but Adam, by disclosing Simon's secret, had precipitated it.

Expecting a call from Simon that evening, she was tense throughout the silent dinner she shared with Adam; she managed to relax a little when Beryl came in to say he had left a message asking her to go riding with him the next morning.

"Will you?" Adam when they were alone again.

"No. But I'll go to the stables and see him."

"He'll probably feel like punching me," Adam said dryly. "I'll have to make my peace with him."

"There's no need for you to apologise to him." Her tone was short. "He deserved it."

The following morning, wearing a cream linen dress only a shade paler than her face, Sharon went to meet

Simon. If only the next few minutes could be magically erased!

Simon regarded her in surprise and she shrugged.

"I'm not going to ride with you. I want to talk to you."

In silence he re-stabled the horses and led her to a bench in the garden. They were sheltered by rosebushes from behind, and front of them a small lily pond glittered in the sunshine.

"Tell me what I've done," he said.

"It's what you haven't done." She stared at him, feeling nothing but compassion. "Why didn't you tell me you're married?"

Colour patchworked his face, making his eyes seem bluer than ever.

"I was going to, you have to believe that. But I couldn't bring myself to do it yesterday." His colour intensified. "Did Adam tell you, or was it Helen?"

"Adam. But you can't blame him," she said quickly. "You were putting him in an impossible position. He didn't mean to tell me, either, but we had an argument and he lost his temper. He was sorry the minute he'd told me, but by then it was too late."

Simon lowered his head into his hands.

"I don't suppose you can forgive me?"

"Of course I forgive you. But it would have been easier for both of us if you'd told me the truth at the beginning. It wouldn't have made any difference, though. I don't love you and I could never marry you."

"You weren't so positive yesterday," he muttered.

"Because I was upset about something else. I tried to

make myself believe it would work, but deep down I knew it wouldn't."

"I'm getting a divorce," he said. "I swear it."

"It won't make any difference."

"You're very unforgiving." His tone made it clear he believed her to be angry at his lie. "A person can make a mistake, you know."

How well she knew it! But she dared not say so.

"You'll thank me one day, Simon. You deserve a woman who genuinely loves you."

"Thanks."

He rose. His fair hair glinted in the bright light and she wondered if the real Sharon Peters would have fallen for him. She liked blond men. Or had she only married Rufus because of his rich family? She was tough and premeditated enough to do that.

"I won't continue working for Adam," Simon interrupted her thoughts. "I'd better tell him."

"Don't leave because of me. I won't be staying here much longer."

"I'll still associate you with this house. That's why I couldn't stay. I have to cut you right out of my mind."

"Time will help," she assured him, and hoped she was right; for then it would also help her.

Unaccountably depressed, she remained in the garden long after Simon had gone, only returning to the house when it was time for lunch.

Beryl met her at the front door. "I was just coming to look for you. You're wanted on the telephone."

Instantly Sharon knew who it was and she ran to the library to take the call.

"What the hell are you playing at?" a hard voice demanded. "I told you I wanted some action in two weeks and—"

"Mrs. Peters has been very ill." Sharon turned her head a movement in the hall. She recognised Adam's tread and lowered her voice. "I can't talk now. Someone might overhear."

"Do you think I care!"

"Let me call you back," Sharon pleaded.

"Not likely! I'm fed up waiting for you. Come and see me tomorrow morning and bring some good news with you. If you don't, I'll come there and shatter everyone's illusions!"

"There's no point in my coming to see you. I've nothing more to tell you."

"Then you'd better work fast. I'll expect you tomorrow!"

The door opened and Sharon hurriedly replaced the receiver as Adam came in.

"I—er—had a phone call," she stammered.

"There's a phone in the hall," he said.

"I didn't know this room was sacred to you." She walked past him to the door.

"Have you seen Simon yet?" he asked.

"Yes. It's all over."

"I'm sorry I had to be the one to shatter your romance."

"Forget it," she said shortly.

"You're going to miss your rides in the morning, aren't you?"

Her smile was bitter. "How do you know I won't miss Simon, too?"

"I don't think you're capable of missing a man," he said harshly. "Only the things he can give you."

"And you can give me so much more, can't you, Adam?"

She almost asked him there and then to increase the allowance, and only the silent sobs constricting her throat prevented her from doing so.

"You may ride with me, if you wish," he said expressionlessly. "I go for a canter at seven-thirty."

"No, thanks. I don't want to spoil your pleasure."

"You won't. Besides, if Mother hears you're not riding with Simon, she'll be upset if you don't come with me."

"Is that an order?" she asked.

"Yes."

"I can't make tomorrow," she said flatly. "I'm going to London."

"A date with your South African friend?"

"Yes."

"You still won't tell me who it is?"

"No," she replied, closing the door behind her.

At ten the next morning Sharon was in the Palace Park Hotel facing the woman she was impersonating. She had left the house an hour before the train for London was due to leave the station, so adamant had she been not to make the journey with Adam, and her nerves were frayed to breaking point.

"I have no news for you, and my coming here is a waste of time," she stated. "Mrs. Peters was very ill last week and I had no chance to talk to Adam."

"She'll have another heart attack if you don't do as you promised. Do you think I like hanging around here, wasting my time?"

"Talk to Adam yourself," Sharon cried. "You're tough enough to deal with him!"

"I'll deal better with his mother."

"You can't!"

"You know how to stop me. Get me an assurance in writing that the old girl has put me in her will and that Adam has doubled my allowance."

"How can I do that?" sighed Sharon.

"Ask him! Tell him you want to go back to Africa and buy some property there. If he won't do it, threaten to tell his mother about the sort of man your loving husband was."

"I can't!" Sharon almost sobbed the words. "I just can't."

"Then I'll come down and do it myself. You've got till Friday. That's my last word." She held open the door and Sharon walked through it, feeling as though she was on her way to the death chamber.

CHAPTER THIRTEEN

SHARON left the hotel in a daze. She had to go somewhere quiet and think; she had to decide what was the best thing to do in the circumstances.

She moved to the kerb, waiting for a break in the traffic before crossing the road. There was a touch on her arm and she swung around and saw Helen Ferrer, looking unfamiliar in a black town suit.

"Hello, Sharon! What are you doing in London?" she exclaimed.

"I came to see a friend."

"The same one you came to see before?"

"I have more than one friend," Sharon replied evenly.

"I'm sure you have," Helen smiled sweetly. "How about joining me for coffee?"

"No, thanks. I have to get back."

"You're not far from the station and you've an hour before the next train. You'll wind up having to hang about and kick your heels on the platform."

Unable to think of an excuse that would not sound deliberately rude, Sharon nodded. She was disconcerted when Helen turned towards the hotel.

"Why don't we go to a café?" Sharon said jerkily.

"The hotel's much nicer. Or don't you want to bump into your friend? By the way, is it a man or a woman?"

"A woman."

"I'm surprised you didn't tell me you'd forgotten! You seem to find your amnesia most convenient."

Sharon moved back towards the kerb. "I don't think having coffee with you is a good idea."

"It's an excellent idea. I've several things to say to you, and I've been waiting for a chance to do so."

Silently Sharon followed Helen into the hotel, but as the older girl headed for the coffee shop, she found it impossible to do as she wanted.

"I don't want a drink," she gasped. "Say what you have to say and then let me go."

"Let you go?" Helen looked amused. "How like a little girl you sound. You really are a marvellous actress." She moved towards a vacant settee in the lobby and sat down. "What I have to say won't take long." Small white teeth nibbled on her full lower lip. "How much longer are you planning to stay at Green Spinney?"

"I—I don't know."

"I want you to leave now. I'll make it worth your while if you do."

Sharon could not believe she had heard correctly.

"If I needed money that badly," she said in a shaky voice, "I could do much better by staying on with my —with Mrs. Peters."

"It's not Mrs. Peters you're concerned with!" Helen almost spat out the words. "It's Adam. Don't think you can fool me. You've fallen for him and you're out to get him!" Sharon half rose, but Helen put out a restraining hand. "You won't get him, though. He despises you."

"Then why are you so scared that you feel you have to offer me money to leave?"

"Because Adam might just be foolish enough to have an affair with you. He's lusting after you like a—"

"Stop it!" Sharon's voice rose and a couple of passers-by stared at her. Lowering her head, she swallowed hard. "How can you say such things about him? I thought you loved him."

"I do. But I also know him. He's a sensual, passionate man and you've aroused him."

"Are you admitting he doesn't love you?"

Helen's slim shoulders moved disdainfully. "Until you came into his life, Adam was almost sure he wanted to marry me. We have the same interests and the same outlook. My family is a good one and I would make him the right sort of wife."

"How coldblooded you are!"

"Because I'm being logical? It's only in recent years that romance has come into marriage. Before that, in our social circle the marriages were arranged."

"Adam would never want that sort of marriage," Sharon protested.

"He'd never want your sort, either. That's why he may be prepared to have an affair with you. It's the best way for him to get you out of his system."

"Why don't you let him do it, then?" Sharon decided to head an attack of her own. "Or are you afraid he might not get me out of his system?"

"Let's say I'm suddenly in a rush to marry him myself. And that won't happen until you've gone out of his life."

"I'll go when it suits me," retorted Sharon.

"You'll go now. This week." Helen looked at the

reception desk. "It won't take me long to find out who you're meeting here. You don't think I believe it's a woman, do you? If it was, you'd have told Adam about her, instead of being so secretive."

"I have my reasons," Sharon murmured, but she knew nothing she said now would dissuade Helen from her vicious plan.

"You have until the end of the week to leave," Helen repeated. "If you're still at the house by then, I'll tell Mrs. Peters the sort of person you are."

"I'm not meeting a man here," said Sharon, leaning forward. "I swear it."

"I'll still tell Mrs. Peters the sort of girl her golden boy married. And once she knows that, you can kiss any money goodbye."

"I don't care about the money," Sharon cried, quite certain Helen didn't believe her. "If you tell Mrs. Peters about me, Adam will never forgive you."

"He won't know," Helen said complacently. "All he'll have to go on is a typed letter sent from London."

Sharon's throat tightened. "An anonymous letter? You—you'd send an anonymous letter? Why, you—!" She drew a deep breath to steady herself. "If you did that, I'd tell Adam it was you."

"You don't think he'd believe you, do you? He'd think one of your men friends had sent it."

"You're evil!" Sharon whispered. "You don't even care that the shock of getting such a letter could kill Mrs. Peters."

"She's tougher than everyone thinks," Helen said scornfully. "Besides, she's old and she's had her life.

Mine's yet to come and I'm tired of waiting. So it's up to you. If you want to protect your mother-in-law, get out." The red mouth twisted. "Once you leave Green Spinney you can do as you like. I don't care if you have a dozen boy-friends or if you've got your memory back and want to go on pretending you haven't. I don't even care if you get Mrs. Peters to leave you all her money. All I care about is Adam." She rose. "That's all I have to say. You know what you must do."

Alone on the settee, Sharon slumped in her chair. So now two women had ordered her to leave Green Spinney by the end of the week! And of the two threats, Helen's was the one she couldn't parry. Sharon Peters might be persuaded to wait a little longer before achieving her mercenary ambitions, but nothing would prevent Helen from coming back to the hotel to ferret out the truth. Should she ask the South African woman to stay at another hotel? It might put Helen off for a while, but inevitably she would uncover something that would lead her to the realisation that the girl at Green Spinney was an impostor.

The only solution was to tell Adam the whole truth as she knew it, and leave him to deal with his sister-in-law as he saw fit. If he wanted to continue buying her silence about Rufus and paying for her to stay away from his mother, then the prerogative was his. She realised that now. She had been foolish in the extreme to act on his behalf. Once she had learned of the real Sharon Peters, she should have confessed her own identity.

Sighing heavily, she left the hotel. Had she not been in love with Adam, there would have been far less difficulty in telling him the truth, but because she still desperately wanted him, she had played for time. But time was no longer on her side. Helen had made that abundantly clear.

Helen. The name was like a canker inside her. How could anyone with normal human warmth threaten to break an old lady's heart? She was even worse than Adam's real sister-in-law, for the woman had never met Mrs. Peters, whereas Helen had known her—and supposedly loved her—since childhood.

Still immersed in painful thoughts, Sharon went on walking. She was halfway down Park Lane when a bus drew abreast. Plastered on its side was an advertisement for a West End play, and the name of the star was directly in her line of vision. Tim Jackman.

Tim! She was reminded of the letter. Why hadn't she tried to find out from Sharon Peters who he was? Without further thought she rushed headlong towards Marble Arch and the nearest tube entrance, where she would find a telephone booth.

Luckily the woman was still in her room at the hotel, but she denied all knowledge of anyone called Tim.

"He must be a particular friend of yours," she added. "You obviously knew him well enough to give him your address over here."

"That means I must trust him," insisted Sharon. "Do you think he's someone I knew at music college?"

"How would I know? You weren't a friend of mine."

"You know me well enough to trust me to come here and take your place."

There was a momentary silence.

"How *did* we know each other?" Sharon asked. "As you just said, we aren't friends."

"We met at a party." The hard voice sounded slightly placatory. "You were playing the piano there—to earn yourself some cash, I suppose. Your having the same name as me set the ball rolling. I found out you needed money; the rest you know."

"And I never spoke of anyone called Tim?"

"'Fraid not. What did the letter say?"

"Not much." Sharon was reluctant to divulge its contents.

"He was probably a boy-friend of yours," the woman said flatly. "You're pretty and I bet you had plenty."

With a feeling of hopelessness Sharon returned to Green Spinney. She could not get Tim out of her mind, convinced that here lay a vital link to her past. But no matter how she searched her memory no clue came to the surface.

It was too late for lunch by the time she reached the house. A quick peep into Mrs. Peters's room told her the woman was resting, and she retired to her own room to do the same.

Lying on her bed, she forced herself to relax, hoping her subconscious would come into play and reveal some spark that would serve to light up the darkness of her memory. But all that happened was that she fell asleep and did not awaken till five-thirty.

Having missed lunch as well as tea, she was decidedly peckish, and after a quick shower and change into a voile dress of misty lilac that enhanced her slender frame, she went down to the kitchen for a cup of tea, gratefully accepting a large slice of freshly baked cake from the cook, a middle-aged woman who had been with the family for years. Her unease at being waited on had long since told Sharon she was not used to a life of luxury common to so many white South African women, and her agreeing to come here for a thousand pounds proved it.

After wiping crumbs from her fingers, she wandered into the drawing room, stopping at the sight of the frail figure on the sofa.

"Mrs. Peters!" she exclaimed. "I'd no idea you were up."

"I thought I'd give you a surprise." The old lady smiled. "You don't know how tired I was of staying in my room." She patted the sofa. "Come and tell me what you did in London."

"Nothing much."

"You didn't go to the hairdresser, did you?"

"No. I went to see a friend."

"I didn't know you had any friends in London. Was it someone you knew in South Africa?"

Sharon's heart began to thump. What on earth had made her say she had gone to meet a friend? Yet she had given herself a golden opportunity to confess the truth. If she could phrase it carefully, if she disclosed only part of the story . . . She moistened her lips.

"There's something I want to tell you," she began. "I'm—"

"Sharon!"

Her name rang out like a shot and she gasped as Adam suddenly materialised beside her, his face grim.

"Darling," his mother protested, "you gave us quite a fright coming in like that!"

"Sorry," he said abruptly, "but—er—Sharon's wanted on the phone."

At once Sharon went into the hall. The receiver was on its hook and when she picked it up she heard the dial tone. Puzzled, she replaced it, and only then realised that Adam was standing right behind her.

"I just wanted to get you out of the room," he explained. "You were going to tell my mother you were leaving, weren't you?"

She hesitated, wondering what he would say if she told him she had been going to disclose much more than that.

"How dare you break your promise?" he went on, keeping his voice low but not disguising its fury. "You gave me your word you'd stay here still she was better."

"She's as well as she'll ever be," Sharon said desperately. "I can't stay on any longer."

"You'll stay till I give you permission to leave!"

She opened her mouth to answer him and then closed it again. Whatever she said would be pointless in the face of the letter she intended to write to him.

She backed away from his imposing presence. At last she had the complete solution. Writing the truth was a coward's way out, but it would be less of an ordeal for her; and by the time he had the letter in his hand, she would be away.

"Well?" he grated. "Have I made myself clear?"

"Abundantly."

Sidestepping him, she ran across the hall and opened the drawing-room door, knowing that as long as she remained at his mother's side he would not quarrel with her.

CHAPTER FOURTEEN

ALONE in her room that night Sharon tried to compose her letter to Adam. It was difficult to write, and after two attempts she gave it up and decided to wait till the following morning. Then she would be fresh and better able to think.

But in the morning another letter from the unknown Tim revived her hopes of being able to discover more about herself and her reasons for agreeing to do an impersonation that filled her with self-disgust.

The letter read:

How come we haven't heard from you? I thought you would be home long before this or would at least have dropped me a note telling me how things were going. Carol and I are worried, so pick up a pen or phone us. I hope you aren't going on with the act, for now there's no need. As I said in my last letter, you're free, Sharon. So come back home where you belong.

Home—where she belonged. Exasperation engulfed her. If only Tim had thought to put his address or telephone number on the letter, she might have stood a chance of finding out exactly where that home was.

Puzzling over the implications of the letter, she was still there when Simon telephoned and asked to see her.

"It won't do any good," she said.

"I'd still like to talk to you. I promise I won't keep

you for long. I'll be waiting for you in the rose garden, half an hour from now."

Wondering what he had to say, she wandered out to the garden. Simon and his problems seemed unimportant compared with her own, and she was vaguely irritated that he could not accept her refusal of him.

A few minutes earlier than he had said, he crossed the lawn to meet her. He looked blond and ruddy as ever, his clear eyes giving no evidence of lack of sleep. Her conscience ceased to trouble her; if he was pining for her, it certainly didn't show.

"I couldn't leave without saying goodbye to you," he began abruptly.

"Where are you going?" she asked.

"I've found another job. I told you I couldn't stay on here."

"Does Adam know?"

"Not yet." He looked deep into her face as if trying to commit it to memory. "Isn't there any hope for me?"

She shook her head. "It wouldn't work. Besides, I'm going back to Africa."

"I didn't think Adam would let you go."

"He can't wait until I do."

Simon shook his head. "It doesn't make sense. I've seen the way he looks at you when he thinks no one's watching him. He—"

"Stop it, Simon!" she begged. "I don't want to talk about Adam."

"Neither do I." Simon held out his hand. "Do I merit a goodbye kiss?"

She longed to refuse, but knew he would be hurt if

she did. Acquiescing, she lifted her face, half turning her cheek to him.

But that was not the sort of kiss he had in mind. With a grunt he grasped her by the forearms and pulled her against his chest. His lips fastened on hers. She gasped and tried to draw back, but his hold was a band of steel.

"Sharon," he said thickly, running his hands up and down her back. They were hot against her skin, but no hotter than the mouth that was trying to force her lips apart. Afraid to open her mouth to yell, she struggled silently, trying to kick him, beating upon his shoulders.

"Let her go, damn you!"

It was a hoarse command, holding so much venom that Simon's arms immediately dropped to his sides. Sharon stumbled and sank on to the bench. She didn't need to look around to know it was Adam.

"I was just saying goodbye," Simon said. "I'm leaving. But before you blow off steam, let me say that I've made arrangements for another bailiff to take over from me."

"I don't need you to start employing people for me!"

"It's Ted Wilcox." Simon was stoical. "You said yourself you'd like to get hold of him if ever I left."

"I see." Some of Adam's anger lessened. "I don't intend saying goodbye to you here. Come to the house before you go."

"Fine. I'll be over later today." Simon bent towards the bench. "Goodbye, Sharon, and good luck."

"Goodbye." she whispered, and waited till he was out of sight before rising.

"You can leave, too," Adam said abruptly. "The sooner the better."

"Yesterday you—"

"That was yesterday. Today I've changed my mind. I don't want you in my home any longer."

"Very well. I'll pack right away." She rose and, hoping her legs would carry her, started to walk across the lawn.

"Before you leave the house, I've a few other things to say to you," he called.

Wearily she rubbed her hand over her forehead, surprised to find it damp.

"Can't we do it now?" she asked.

"No. I have a business appointment. But there are some questions that need answering and you're the only person who can do it. I'll be back within an hour, if that's all right with you."

"I'm yours to command," she said bitterly, and turned away.

But once in her room she could not face the prospect of another battle with him. For that was what it would become. He had never believed her amnesia was real and would try to force her to tell the truth.

Well, he didn't need to use force. She would tell him the whole truth as far as she knew it. In fact, hindsight made her think she had been crazy not to have done so as soon as she had returned from seeing his real sister-in-law. She should have let Adam deal with the woman instead of trying to play for time until Mrs. Peters had recovered.

Sitting at the bureau, she began to write hurriedly.

"Dear Adam—"

How cold the words looked when what she really

meant was, "Darling Adam, my very own darling Adam."

She shook her head and fixed her mind on what she wanted to say.

I can't face another meeting with you. Anyway, it isn't necessary. I don't know what you want to ask me, but I'm sure that what I have to tell you will answer most of your questions.

My name is Sharon Moore and I'm not Rufus's widow. I agreed to come here and pretend I was, for a thousand pounds. Your sister-in-law knew she wouldn't make a good impression on your mother, which is why she engaged me. I was supposed to worm my way into her affections and make sure she made me a beneficiary in her will. I was also supposed to make you give me a bigger allowance.

Despite what you believe, I really don't remember anything about myself and it was a great shock to discover I wasn't Sharon Peters. I still don't know my background, only my name—the little bit your sister-in-law has told me.

She was the person who telephoned me at dinner the other night, and the one I went to see in London; so I wasn't meeting a boy-friend, as you thought. When she told me why I was at Green Spinney, I planned to leave at once, but your mother had a heart attack and I was forced to stay. But in any event I'd made up my mind to go this Friday and leave you a letter telling you the whole story.

Your asking me to go this morning has only precipitated matters by a few days. You see, I'd realised I couldn't carry out your sister-in-law's plans. I know I agreed to them, but I can't think why. I'd never do such a thing no matter how much money I was offered. But I don't expect you to believe me.

Sharon paused here, her eyes too blinded by tears to see the page. She wiped them away with the back of her hand and then continued.

You're the only one who can deal with the situation now. You're a strong-minded person and maybe you can frighten your sister-in-law off. She's everything you believe her to be—and worse. So you were right to hate what I stood for!

The one thing I want you to believe is that I became very fond of your mother and wouldn't do anything to hurt her. But even if you had let me stay on here—for her sake—I think it would have ended in disaster. Sharon Peters is a greedy woman and will go on making more and more demands.

There were other things she could have said, but they would have given away too much of her personal feelings, so she signed the letter and placed it in an envelope.

Then she started to pack, bundling her clothes uncaringly into her case. She longed to say goodbye to Mrs. Peters, but knew it was out of the question.

One by one she carried her cases down to the hall and then telephoned for a taxi, stressing that it was wanted urgently. She had to be away from the house before Adam returned, and that left her with a bare fifteen-minute margin.

Nervously she paced the floor, breathing a sigh of relief as a dilapidated car chugged to a stop outside the front door. She was in the act of climbing into it when Beryl appeared at the top of the steps, her face mirroring her astonishment.

"Mrs. Rufus!" she exclaimed. "Where are you going?"

"I'm leaving. But don't say anything to my—to Mrs. Peters."

"But why are you going?" The girl looked extremely upset. "Does Mr. Adam know? I'm sure he wouldn't want—"

"Please, Beryl!" Sharon cut her short. "I don't want to miss my train. I've left a note for Mr. Adam in the library. And I've left you a little present in my bedroom. I hope you'll think of me when you wear it."

"I don't need a present to remember you by," Beryl said tearfully, running down the steps. "Are you sure you should be going? You look ever so pale." Extracting herself from the girl's grasp, Sharon eased herself into the car and firmly ordered the driver to set off for the train station; she waved with resolute cheeriness until they had rounded a bend in the drive and were out of sight of the house. Only then did she let her mask drop, and she huddled in her seat, trying not to picture how Adam's face would look when he read her letter.

CHAPTER FIFTEEN

DURING the journey to London Sharon tried to make plans for her future. The first thing was to go to South Africa House and talk to one of the officials. It might be possible for him to initiate enquiries about her in Cape Town and see if she had any relatives. The airline company was also a source she could tap. Her amnesia was a result of the plane crash, and they were surely responsible for her welfare.

If Adam had not come to the hospital and taken over her life, she would have thought of doing these two things immediately. But living at Green Spinney had somehow made her incapable of thinking clearly. Or perhaps it was her love for Adam that had held her in chains, for fear she would learn things about herself that would have made him despise her even more than he already did.

Arriving in London, she hailed a taxi and asked to be taken to an inexpensive hotel, where she deposited her luggage before going to South Africa House.

The official she dealt with there could not have been more helpful. To begin with, he questioned her delay in not coming to them earlier and she carefully sketched in some of her reasons, explaining she had been living with an English family who had believed that she was a relative.

"But now I know I'm not," she concluded, and showed him the letter from the mysterious Tim.

"You've no idea what his surname is?" the official asked.

"Not a clue."

"*He* could be your family. He doesn't sound like a boy-friend—not when he mentions another woman called Carol!" Seeing Sharon's abashed expression, the man smiled.

"I suppose you're wondering why you never thought of that yourself? If you hang on, I'll have a look in a Cape Town directory."

Excitement kept Sharon pacing the small room until he returned bearing a sheet of paper with some addresses and phone numbers on it.

"There are several T. Moores listed," he said, "and lots of Thomases, but only one Timothy."

Sharon tried to speak but couldn't, and the man gently pushed her on to a chair. "I suggest you call up Timothy Moore first," he went on. "If he isn't the one who wrote the letters, you could try a few of the others."

"Won't that be expensive?" she queried.

"The airline will meet all your costs. Didn't the family you were staying with tell you that?"

She shook her head. "Adam—Mr. Peters—said nothing about it. I took it for granted I was his sister-in-law and that the airline had no reason to deal with me."

"Well, now you know you're not Mrs. Peters, I'm sure they'll make themselves responsible for you. But let's telephone Timothy Moore in Cape Town first."

Realising she was too overwrought to make the call, the official did it for her. There was no answer from the other end and the man explained that many firms had closed for summer vacation and that the unknown Timothy could have gone away on holiday.

"You could call again later," he added, "and in the meantime I'll make an appointment for you to see one of the airline representatives. I may not be able to arrange it for today, though."

"Here's where I'm staying." She gave him her address, which he noted down and, with his promise to call her as soon as he had any news, she headed back to her hotel. She stopped at a little café next door to the hotel for a cup of coffee and a roll. She tried not to think ahead, afraid this might increase her despondency. What would happen if Tim could not be traced, if her memory failed to return and she was faced with having to build a new life for herself without ever recollecting the past? As always, such thoughts set her trembling, and she shakily left the coffee shop and entered the foyer of the hotel. She walked towards the reception clerk to collect her key. She was almost at the desk when a tall, wide-shouldered man rose from a chair. Fear held her motionless, though she still had control of her voice.

"H–how did you find me?' she stammered. "What do you want?"

"To talk to you. I called South Africa House and they gave me this address." Adam had a firm hold of her arm, making flight impossible.

"Have you seen your sister-in-law yet?" she asked.

"No. My first concern was to find you."

"Why?"

"To settle some more important matters."

"I've told you everything I know." Sharon sat on the edge of the chair into which Adam had pushed her, wondering if escape was possible.

"I can't answer any questions," she said, "because I don't remember anything about myself. All I know is that my name is Sharon Moore."

"You've no idea how you became mixed up with my sister-in-law?"

"For the money—I told you in my letter."

"It doesn't make sense," he argued.

"I'd have thought it made perfect sense to you. Don't I strike you as the sort of person who'd lie and cheat for a thousand pounds?"

Anger brought her to her feet and before he could prevent her, she raced across the foyer.

"Sharon!" he called.

She refused to listen and pushed open the glass door to the outside.

"Sharon!" Adam called her again, and she sped into the road, desperate to escape him. An empty taxi was cruising past and she was so intent to get into it before Adam reached her that she didn't see the cyclist coming in the opposite direction. The front wheel hit her in the side, sending her staggering backward. She flung her arms out to protect herself from falling, but it was too late. Her shoulder struck the pavement, taking the brunt of the blow before her head. But the impact of the curb on her temple was still enough to shatter her consciousness. Third time unlucky, she thought in that split second, and then she knew no more.

When she opened her eyes she was lying in a darkened room. A tentative turn of her head told her it was her hotel bedroom, and a tentative movement of her body advised her to remain where she was for a bit longer.

"You'll have a headache," Adam's voice said, "but the doctor has assured me there are no bones broken."

With a gasp she forced herself into a sitting position. Adam was ensconced in the one armchair the room possessed. He had discarded his jacket, and the tray by his side, with its assortment of tureens and coffee pot, told her some considerable time had passed.

"Go away," she croaked. The room was blurring again but she held on to reality as best she could. "Leave me alone, Adam. We've nothing to say."

"Lie still and rest." His hands were upon her body: strong, warm hands that held her down. "Sleep some more, Sharon. You'll feel better when you wake up next time."

It was too much effort to argue, apart from which her tongue was leaden in her mouth, making speech impossible. She closed her eyes and enjoyed the floating feeling washing over her. Adam was right. There would be time to talk later.

When she awoke for the second time it was dark outside the window, though in her room a small lamp shed muted radiance in the far corner. But the most important thing was that Adam had gone.

She sat up gingerly. There was no dizziness and she swung her legs to the floor. Apart from a slight stiffness in her shoulder she felt normal. It was a good thing the Moore family came from strong stock. She smiled, remembering that Tim was fond of saying this each time the twins hurt themselves.

The twins! Tim! She clutched at the bedhead. Her brother, Tim. She remembered now. Remembered it all. Sobbing with relief, she crossed to the dressing table and stared at herself. She wasn't just a name any longer; she was a person with a past and a present. Resolutely she refused to contemplate that without Adam she had no future. Suffice it that she had regained her memory. Miracles were not for mortals to create.

She opened her bag and took out the two letters she had received from her brother. No wonder he hadn't called her to find out how she was: to have done so might have endangered her masquerade—a masquerade she had entered because of him. Yet both his letters had made it clear she could end her pretence whenever she liked—if only she had been in a mental position to have realised this.

But now everything was falling into place. At last she could face Adam without shame. What she had done was wrong but, knowing her motivations, not unforgivable.

She was engulfed by such a warm feeling of happiness that her body broke out in a sweat, and with trembling legs, she returned to the bed and sank down on it. For several moments she stayed there, collecting her thoughts and satisfying herself that her memory had indeed returned. She found no blanks anywhere. Everything was clear: her departure from South Africa, the plane crash, the struggle to escape from the burning wreck. She shied away from this last thought and went into the spartan bathroom to wash—as if water could expunge that particular memory!

Her face was pale, her dishevelled hair a golden aureole around her head. Washing hurriedly, she applied lipstick and mascara. The colour heightened her fragility, making her eyes luminous and large, her mouth a sensual scarlet focus. Nervously she rubbed off the lipstick and went back into the bedroom.

Adam was there, formally attired in a suit, his tanned face set in impassive lines.

"Feeling more like yourself?" he asked.

"I'm completely myself, thank you."

Her tone, as much as her words, made his eyes narrow, and she noticed the dark shadows beneath them.

"I know who I am and why I'm here," she went on breathlessly. "It wasn't for the money. In fact, there wasn't any money involved in it for me. Your sister-in-law made up that part of it."

"I know."

"You do?" Sharon gasped. "How?"

"I've just spoken to your brother in Cape Town and he told me the whole story."

Sharon's legs refused to support her and she looked at the chair.

Intercepting her glance, Adam reached out with both hands and drew her forward and down on to the bed. Then slowly, he sat beside her. His thigh touched hers, but she lacked the strength to move away. How could she when all she wanted to do was press even closer?

"Tim has told me the whole story," Adam went on and, in dispassionate tones, put the entire episode of

Tim and the real Sharon Peters in perspective. He began with Carol, Tim's wife, and her obsessive devotion to the twins, born a year earlier, lightly touching on Tim's feeling that he was no longer important to the woman he loved nor even necessary in his own home.

"Tim needed a lot of support himself, at that time," Sharon said in firm defence of her brother. "He'd started up his own hi-fi business and wanted to be able to talk things over with Carol. But she never had time for him. That's when he met your sister-in-law. He'd gone to install some stereo equipment in her home and she fell for him. He's very good-looking and—"

"He must be if he takes after you," Adam interposed.

"But the affair lasted only a couple of weeks," Sharon continued as if she had not heard him. "By then he came to his senses and realised what a fool he'd been."

"Which was too late, of course," Adam concluded, "because by then he had written a couple of stupid letters to that bitch of a woman and she was threatening to tell Carol."

Sharon's eyes darkened with pain as she remembered the misery Tim had gone through in his efforts to buy those letters back. But Sharon Peters had enjoyed her power to blackmail and her demands had increased rather than lessened with time. It was when those demands become unbearable that Tim had finally confessed the whole sordid episode to his sister.

"I went to see her myself," Sharon stated flatly, "but she said she would only give Tim back his letters if I went to London and impersonated her for a few months.

I told you her reasons for my doing that in the letter I left you."

"It's all so clear now that you've explained it," Adam breathed. "I blame myself for not tackling you the moment I discovered you were an impostor."

Sharon stared at him, not sure she had heard correctly.

"You mean—you—knew I wasn't—that I was—" she gasped.

"I didn't know who you were, but I damn well knew you weren't Sharon Peters!"

"How?"

"Because of your hair."

She touched her hand to it. "I don't follow."

"It's quite simple." He lifted his own hand towards her hair, as if he wanted to touch it, too. Then he dropped his arm and half moved away from her, yet still remained close enough for her to see the faint rise and fall of his chest. "I knew that my sister-in-law was a dyed blonde—Rufus told me so in one of his letters. Apparently he wanted her to go back to being a brunette, but she wouldn't. It wasn't the complete proof I needed, but I soon had more evidence."

"I'm younger," she said quickly.

He chuckled. It was the first time he had relaxed this much with her and she was dismayed at the way it disarmed her.

"You're much younger," he agreed, "and much more innocent, too! But that wasn't what I meant. It was when I heard you playing the piano. That's when I knew for sure that you were an impostor. You see, Rufus was crazy about music and he had told me that the only thing that bothered him about his new wife was that she was tone-deaf! That was when he'd first married her, of course. Shortly before he died he had lost all his illusions about her."

There was a short silence; both of them were preoccupied with their own thoughts.

"Then I went through all this for nothing!" Sharon let out a deep breath. "But why didn't you confront me with the truth and throw me out?"

"Because it was already too late. You have a marked ability to wrap yourself around a man's heart and—" The intensity of his gaze set her heart racing; but he started to speak again and she forced herself to concentrate.

"At one time I thought that perhaps my sister-in-law was dead and that you'd taken over her identity in order to live off Rufus's family. But as I came to know you better, I couldn't believe you'd be willing to live a lie for the rest of your life."

"How right you were!" Her mouth twisted as she recollected the anguish she had undergone in the short while she had known she was doing the impersonation at all.

"You'll never know the battle I fought with myself," he went on, abruptly rising and going to the window. "I hated you, yet at the same time I wanted you. And when you went out with Simon I could have throttled you both!"

"I knew you were jealous," she admitted.

"I couldn't tell you how I felt, though. You were living in my home as Rufus's wife, and until I knew the reason—and also if you had really lost your memory

—I was forced to keep quiet. Then this morning, when you ran away, nothing mattered to me except finding you again."

He turned and walked back across the room, but this time he knelt by the side of the bed. His face was brought level with hers, and he was able to stare deep into her eyes.

"I love you, my darling. That's why I came after you —to tell you I loved you and didn't care a damn about you impersonating my sister-in-law for the money. I felt sure you must have had a valid reason for doing it."

"You honestly believed that? That it wasn't because I wanted money for my career?"

"I didn't think you'd ever do anything underhanded merely to further your ambitions. I knew it had to be for some emotional or moral reason."

"How right," she said shakily. "I was so afraid Carol would leave Tim if she discovered he'd been unfaithful to her."

"I'm glad he came clean," said Adam. "His wife had to know the truth. You can't be happy together if your marriage is built on a lie. Apart from which I think your own sister-in-law needed to know you can't discard a husband once he's given you some children to love, and then expect the man to hang around until you've ready to accept him again. Women don't want to be regarded as sex symbols," he added dryly, "and men don't want to be only seen as studs!"

Pink of cheek, Sharon nodded, but was careful to avoid his eyes. "What will you do about the real Sharon Peters? If your mother finds out the truth she'll receive an awful shock."

"She has to know—I realise that now. It's the only way of rendering Sharon Peters harmless!"

"Harmless! What a wonderful word. She's such a—"

"Don't try to find the right word," he advised. "I've already seen her, so I know what you mean. That's where I went this afternoon while you were asleep."

He moved lithely and was on the bed again, his arms around Sharon's slender body. "Don't you think we've exhausted the past and should start thinking of the future? You know I won't let you go back to Africa, don't you?"

Sharon still refused to look at him and focused on his shirt. "I wasn't sure."

"What do I have to do to convince you? Didn't my kisses tell you anything?"

"Only that you wanted me."

"Want you for ever," he said fiercely, and tilted her chin with his hand, forcing her to look up. "I want to make love to you. Want to be the only man who has the right to possess you, take care of you for the rest of your life and cherish the children that our love for each other will give us. If that isn't love enough for you," he said thickly, "then tell me what else I must do."

Words failed her and she clung to him. Heat emanated from his body and she responded to it—in the way she knew she would always respond to him. She and Adam were one. The sound and the echo; the violin and the bow.

"Would you have married Helen if you hadn't met me?"

She had not meant to ask the question, but now that it was out, she was glad.

"Probably," he said carelessly. "But you'd have married some other man if you hadn't met me."

She laughed. Trust Adam to be logical and right!"

"I was terribly jealous of her. That's why I went on seeing Simon."

"They're both unimportant." Adam's mouth moved along her cheek but did not touch her lips. "I dare not kiss you. If I do, we'll never get out of this room tonight!"

"I like this room," she whispered, her hands coming up to touch his silky hair. "I'm not afraid of you, Adam."

"You should be. I'm afraid of myself." He pulled her hands away and stood up. "I've paid the bill here and told them we're leaving. I want to take you home. Do you feel up to the journey? If not we can stay over."

"I'd like to go home." Tears filled her eyes. "I never thought I'd hear you say those words to me. I'm so happy, Adam."

"Our happiness is just beginning." He caught the hands she held up to him and gently pulled her to her feet. "But it isn't going to begin here," he said whimsically. "I've a more romantic notion for our honeymoon. A long slow voyage to your family. Say a month on a cruise ship?"

"Lovely!" She nuzzled her face into his neck. "I'm an excellent sailor."

"Pity," he said against her mouth. "I was hoping you'd want to stay in bed all the time!"

Her laughter was stifled by his lips and, returning his kiss, she savoured the joy of the future.

Stories full of intrigue, excitement and romance....

Woven from history's rich tapestry of life, love and adventure, each novel in the Masquerade Historical Romance series emphasizes the timelessness of love through the ages.

You, too, can be transported back to a bygone age of true romance, when deeds were daring and heroes dashing and the smile of a beautiful woman could change the course of history anywhere in the world....

Masquerade titles will be published every month from July.

July Titles

SOPHIE AND THE PRINCE
Sylvia Sark

The sweet and gentle Sophie Johnson travels to pre-revolutionary Russia to be English teacher to the daughters of the dynamic Prince Peter Rasimov. There she falls deeply in love with him, but wonders how she can overcome the difference in their backgrounds and deal with the treachery of the scheming French governess.

THE DEVIL'S DAUGHTER
Marguerite Bell

As companion to his wards, Harriet Yorke does not hesitate to confront the Marquis of Capel when he neglects them. Her appearance at the scene of a duel almost causes his death, but gentle nursing does nothing to make her obstinate patient alter his low opinion of her. Is jealousy the answer?

MADELON
Valentina Luellen

Returning to court in 11th century Spain the beautiful Madelon and her brother Paco are captured by fierce Moors. Almost enslaved, their rescue comes unexpectedly from the noble and magnificent Valentin Maratin, her brother's sworn enemy...

STRANGER AT THE GATE
Frances Lang

After years of exile in Holland, Clemence de Frainville's brother unexpectedly returns to his family château in France. Clemence is initially puzzled when she does not recognise Edouard, and then angered when he forbids her to marry the handsome Armand.

Order your copies now and be among the first to enter our exciting world of historical romance

OLD-FASHIONED VALUE AT 60p net.